WHAT DANCES IN THE DARK

A COLLECTION OF SHORT HORROR STORIES

SHAWN BROOKS

Copyright © [2025] by [Shawn Brooks]

All rights reserved.

No portion of this book may be reproduced in any form without written permission from the publisher or author, except as permitted by U.S. copyright law.

Cover design by Abdullah at Book Cover Hub.

Edited by Heather M. Chuon.

CONTENTS

THE MAN WITH THE GLASS BONES

"The man with the glass bones is going to get you tonight."

"He's gonna come through your window and take you away."

"He'll make your bones just like his. They'll clang like windchimes when you walk."

Chris's face went hot, and he clenched his fists. The other kids surrounded him in a semicircle, laughing and taunting him.

"I don't believe you guys, you're just trying to scare me," he said.

The boy nearest him, Jake, the one with a flat nose and freckled face that looked like a slice of salami, stepped closer. "All new kids get taken, it's a fact. Maybe if your family came in the summer, you'd be fine. Fall is when he gets hungry. Has to get fat for winter. Sorry." He smiled wide but his eyes flashed with menace.

Chris wanted to punch Jake's deli-meat face. He also wanted to run home and cry in his mother's lap. He was on the verge of doing both at the same time.

"Jake, Sinclair, Marshall, what are you three doing?" came the commanding yet soft voice of Mrs. Tennerson. "Is this any way to treat our new friend?"

The boys' faces flushed red. "We weren't doin' nothin'," Jake said, his eyes unable to meet the teacher's.

"Nothing? Well, let's see to it that it stays that way. Run along, you three."

The boys sped away, laughing and pushing each other. Jake turned back and made eye contact with Chris. He ran his forefinger across his throat and stuck out his tongue.

"Christopher, don't you pay them any attention. They're nice boys at heart. It will just take some time, is all, for you to become friends." Mrs. Tennerson patted Chris on his head. She smelled like roses. Her blonde hair caught the sun in a way that made it glow, like a halo. Chris blushed as all the boys blushed when Mrs. Tennerson spoke with them.

"If they bother you again, you come and tell me. All children are special here."

She smiled at him – oh, how that smile made the world melt away – and walked back to her classroom.

Chris leaned back against the slide, nearly in love. But as soon as she left his sight, reality set back in. The air bit his face and made him shiver. But it was much easier to breathe here than back in California. A fact that did nothing to make him like this place more.

Why did Mom have to come here? I hate it.

A cold wind grew harsher and blew across the playground. It picked up dead leaves and scattered them in spirals. The aspens that surrounded the school swayed and creaked. Dozens of kids ran around, chasing each other, screaming and playing games. Chris stood alone by the slide. His fortress against the tides of unknown faces.

Everywhere Chris looked past the school was that forest. The trees with their white trunks and golden leaves looked like bones sticking out of the ground with decaying teeth skewered atop their branches. Mom thought they were beautiful. Not Chris. To him, there was something beneath that beauty, in the dark places between the trees, that unnerved him.

He climbed the stairs and slid down the slide. Of course, he felt ridiculous, doing it by himself. Being a loner. He'd rather be playing handball with the other boys over by the basketball courts. But Jake was an ass. Chris had only been here for a week and that sandwich-faced bully targeted him from the outset.

What did I do wrong?

He put his feet on the ladder again and stopped.

A light ringing sound started coming from the trees. All the other kids were too busy to hear it, but Chris, alone with his thoughts, heard it. Like bells. The sound grew louder until the other kids noticed it too and stopped moving. All faces turned toward the white forest.

He had never heard this before.

The tinkle of the bells turned to a clanging. Then to a wild and chaotic bashing sound that no longer sounded melodic and gentle, but more like the breaking of glass. It sounded like hundreds of panes of glass were being shattered by hammers. Chris clutched the steps of the slide as if a hunk of metal could shield him.

The other kids, though, didn't look scared. They stared out at the forest in silence. No running or crying or screaming.

A voice came on the intercom, "Okay, students, time to come in now. Lunchtime is over."

The teachers on yard duty shepherded the kids back to the classrooms. Everyone walked back calmly. The breaking-glass sound subsided into nothingness.

The gym teacher, Mr. Vicks, came over to the slide. "Chris! Let's go," he barked. Chris followed him and joined the lines of the other students filing back inside. He looked back at the forest beyond the chain-link fence.

For just a moment, he thought he saw a man between the trees

"Honey, just give this place a chance," Mom said, her face buried in her hands, sitting at the dining room table. "It was probably some construction going on. You said it yourself, no one looked like they thought it was weird."

"Why can't we just go back home?" Chris asked. "There's no malls. No movie theaters. Everywhere is just old people and kids."

Mom looked up. Her eyes were ringed with deep purple bags. "Let's just see how it goes for a little longer, okay? I need this job. If everything is still hard after a few more months, I promise you, I'll see if I can get transferred."

Chris cracked open a Mountain Dew and downed it. "Promise?"

"Cross my heart. But you have to promise to try and make this place a home. Try to make some friends."

"The kids at school suck."

Mom ran her fingers through her auburn hair. Chris noticed slight streaks of gray that weren't there just a month ago.

"A friend of mine at work, she has a son in your grade, Tim, I think. Why don't I set up a play date for you guys?"

"Gross, a play date? I'm not five anymore, Mom."

"Okay Mr. Grown-up, call it whatever you want to. I'll talk to Trish and make it happen."

"Mom, please, don't. Everyone already thinks I'm a freak."

She got up and walked over to him, placing her hands on his shoulders. "Okay, forget it for now. Let's get some pizza tonight."

In a flash, all of Chris's problems disappeared.

Mom, how could you?

That sneaky woman told him they were getting pizza. Well, they were at a pizza place, so not totally a liar. But Tim was there too, with his mom.

When did she text and make this happen?

Chris was equal parts angry, embarrassed, and impressed.

"Janet! Oh, this was such a good idea," Trish said.

Mom walked up to the table, and they hugged each other.

Tim was playing with his phone, not looking up. Mom nudged Chris with her foot.

"Hey," Chris said.

"Hey," came the reply.

Their moms sat down, and Chris hesitantly pulled out a chair. The adult conversation was a blur of meaningless background noise. Chris heard something about Tim's older brother going to college in two days. How Tim just joined the soccer league. Blah blah blah.

Neither of the boys spoke. There was pizza, thank God. But it did have mushrooms on it. Chris picked them off his slice and slurped the cheese off the crust. Tim looked up at him like he was an animal.

After several slices were desecrated in such fashion, Mom spoke up. "Hey, you guys go play something at the arcade. Our treat." She handed Chris some money and Trish did the same for Tim.

The boys got up and walked across the tiny pizza parlor to the three machines that Mom somehow thought was an entire arcade.

God, this town sucks.

Neither of the boys attempted small talk. But when Chris saw that even this hole-in-the-wall place had "Exterminator III," he shouted, "Holy shit! I love this game."

He instantly regretted cursing and looked over his shoulder to make sure Mom didn't hear.

Coast clear.

"You do? Me too," Tim said.

All the awkward ice melted away. Chris put in a few coins and they each grabbed a plastic gun. Seconds later, a horde of zombies came out. Chris pulled the trigger and splattered green blood over the screen. Tim even saved Chris once from getting attacked by some monster hyena zombie thing. Laughing. Whispering "Shit" when a big monster came on screen. High fiving each other after beating the evil scientist.

Chris was surprised to hear his Mom's voice saying it was time to go home. Forty minutes had passed, and he didn't even realize it.

"Hey," Tim said. "My brother is having a going-away party tomorrow night. It's gonna be boring and I got some games. Want to come over?"

"Yeah, sounds cool," Chris said. Voice calm and indifferent. Heart exploding with joy.

Chris lay in bed in his dark room. Stomach full of pizza, *sans* mushrooms. He couldn't get to sleep. He was too excited thinking about tomorrow, going over to Tim's. He was a little embarrassed that he was getting all mushy about it. But this was his first friend in this weird town, and he was undeniably happy.

A jingle of bells coming from outside.

The sound was soft, like windchimes.

He'll make your bones just like his. They'll clang like windchimes when you walk.

Chris' heart beat faster. He pulled the blankets up to his face.

The bells were getting closer. They sounded like they were coming from the side of the house, around the corner from where his bedroom was. They drew nearer until they were outside his window.

The sounds stopped.

A wheezing sound. It could have been the wind because it was way too loud for him to be able to hear it inside the house. But it was a rhythmic sound. Like breathing.

"Gef mér sterkann mann ok ek mun gera hann veikan."

The voice was harsh. It grated against Chris's ears like sandpaper. It definitely wasn't English. The words were so foreign to him, he thought it must have been the wind. He was imagining the words.

A jungle of bells. Closer now. Right outside the window. His second-story window.

"Gef mér sterkann mann ok ek mun gera hann veikan."

Not imagination. The voice was clearer now. It almost sounded like it came from inside the room.

He thought he saw a shadow on the other side of his curtains. Impossible, since there was no light source outside to highlight the silhouette.

Silence.

"Mom." His voice came out weak and feeble. It cracked a little.

The sound of cracking glass.

"Veikleiki!"

"Mom!" Chris flung his blankets off and rushed out of the room. He flipped on the hallway lights and ran into his mom's bedroom. He switched on the lights and jumped on her bed.

"What in the?.." Her half-closed eyes and frizzy hair rose out of her mountain of blankets.

"There's somebody outside my window!"

"What? Come on, honey—"

"Mom! I'm serious."

He grabbed her hand and tugged it. She got out of bed and let him take her to his room.

"You have got to stop playing scary games, honey."

He pulled her into his room and turned on the lights.

"There, at the window."

He let go of her hand and she stumbled to the window like a pizza parlor zombie. She opened the curtains.

"No one here."

"Are you sure? What about in the woods?"

She pressed her face to the glass. "Nope. Nothing but a beautiful forest full of scary things like deer and owls." She laughed.

"Mom, I'm ser-i-ous."

"I'm sorry. I'm sure you did hear something, but you're just not used to living by the woods. It was probably an animal."

He thought about arguing with her, but knew it was useless. Maybe he was being a wuss. Mom kissed his forehead, he pushed her away and said, "Yuck," and he went back to the bed. She turned off his light and shut the door.

Mom forgot to close the curtains.

Chris got out of bed and rushed over to the window. He gripped the curtain but stayed a moment, looking outside. The tree line came right up to their backyard. It was too dark to see anything except for the vague shadows of the trees swaying. He laughed to himself.

You're 11 years old, time to grow up, dude.

Before he closed the curtains, he froze.

There, in the bottom left corner of the glass.

A large crack.

Saturday night. Mom drove the old Thunderbird up a long driveway to a massive house. String lights were hung up outside between several large oaks in the front yard. Long tables full of food. Over 20 people were eating, drinking and talking. Mom pulled the car over and got out. Chris followed with his overnight bag.

Tim was waiting on the front porch. Trish came out, hugged Mom and kissed her on the cheek. They chatted away while the boys waited impatiently.

"Okay, honey, I'll see you tomorrow."

And with that, Mom was in the car and driving away.

"Come on, I just got Hellblazers. If we start now, we can beat it by the morning," Tim said.

Before the boys went inside, Trish took hold of Chris's arm. She held on a little too tightly, digging her flashy purple nails into his skin.

"You boys, stay inside tonight. It's Riley's big day." She glared at Chris and then at her son. "Understood?"

"Yes Ma'am," Tim said, face paper white.

"Yes Mom," Chris said by mistake. His face flushed crimson.

Trish smiled a little and let go of his arm. "Good." She then walked off the porch and joined the party outside.

"Dude, what was that about?' Chris asked.

"Nothing. It's just Riley's stupid going away party."

Chris saw a blond guy, maybe in his late teens, standing under the oak smiling. He assumed it was Riley; he looked like the youngest guy there. A pretty blonde woman leaned in and kissed him.

"Holy shit! Is that Mrs. Tennerson?" Chris was more than shocked. He felt betrayed.

"Come on, let's just go play the game," Tim said and led the way to his room.

"Watch out! Get it! Get it!" Tim shouted.

"A man can only do so much," Chris said as he calmly stared at the screen.

A large green monster was rising out of the ground, and they had only two thousand bullets between them. And a nuke bazooka. But they had to conserve and save that for the really tough boss battles. Green monster guy was not that fight.

"No! Shoot it!" Tim bellowed.

The monster raised a claw and swiped down Chris's character. He rolled to the side, took out the nuke, and launched it. An orange glow overtook the screen, followed by a rumbling of the controller. The monster was dead, but at what cost?

"Why'd you waste the missile?" Tim asked.

"I dunno, I had to. I was cornered."

A knock on the door. "Timothy, time to turn off the game and get ready for bed, it's almost 10," Trish said.

"Okay, Mom."

Chris whispered, "I thought you said we could play till midnight."

"Me too."

"So your mom always makes you go to bed early?"

"No, I think it's because of the party. Sorry, I didn't think it would be a big deal."

With that, Tim saved the game and shut it off.

Chris looked on, astonished. If it was his house, he'd just turn the volume down and keep on playing. Tim, though, his face was ashen as he hurriedly packed up the console. He seemed to actually be obeying his mom like she was some kind of drill sergeant. Not his place to make fun of him, not yet at least, he only knew the kid a few days and didn't want to screw things up.

Tim changed into his PJs and dove into his bed. There was a sofa fold-out bed set up for Chris.

"Good night, Chris," Tim said as he reached for the light switch. Chris hadn't even moved to change his clothes yet. Tim clicked the lights off.

"Dude," Chris whispered. "Can you turn the light back on? I can't see my stuff."

"Shut up, man," Tim hissed. "If my mom hears us talking, we'll get in trouble."

End of debate.

Feeling off-balance, Chris groped in the dark for his backpack. After tripping over something on the floor and picking up some of Tim's dirty clothes by accident, he finally found his bag, switched into his sweatpants and hoodie, and climbed into the bed.

He thought about saying goodnight to Tim but held his tongue. The atmosphere shifted from fun monster-bashing to a deadly silence. It felt as though breathing too loud could set something off. With every tick of the mechanical clock in the room, Chris held his breath, imagining Tim's mom bursting in and grabbing his arm too hard again.

He wondered if he should tell his mom about that. He knew it wasn't right. But mom and Trish looked like they got along well, and Trish's husband was mom's boss. He also didn't want to lose his friendship with Tim.

He chose silence.

Chris woke to the bells. Faint and distant, but their metallic ring cut through his dreams. Two chimes rang out about every 10 seconds. Chris looked over towards Tim. It was too dark to see anything, but he could hear Tim breathing heavily, almost snoring.

Ding-ding.

It was almost melodic and soothing. Chris tried to tell himself it was just some windchimes out on the front porch.

Windchimes. Bones like his.

A set of footsteps passed on the other side of Tim's closed door. Chris braced himself, expecting Trish to barge in. The footsteps went down the hall. The wood creaked under their weight. He heard them thump their way down the steps. Then a door opened downstairs, but he never heard it close.

Ding-ding.

The sound was louder now. Chris got out of bed and went to the window. He lifted the curtain and froze. Tim's window was covered in cracks. Hundreds of them. He looked down on the front yard. The string lights still buzzed gold light and food was still out on the tables. But there were no people.

Ding-ding.

The bells sounded like they were coming from somewhere to the right of the yard, around the corner to the backyard, near the tree line of the aspens. Chris looked in that direction and saw a flash of yellow hair lit up by what looked like a flaming torch. Only for a second, and then the figure was gone.

Mrs. Tennerson.

Jealousy filled his heart. He knew she was married and an adult, he wasn't stupid. But he did see her kiss Tim's brother. Not on the cheek like Trish did with Mom, but right on the lips.

Chris knew he shouldn't, but curiosity and unrequited love took hold of him. He walked to the door, being sure to not make a sound. The floorboards creaked loudly, but Tim responded only by rolling over and snoring even louder.

Chris cracked the door open. The squeal of the hinges made him wince. No sound of waking from Tim.

Chris snuck into the dark hallway. A warm light from downstairs cast its glow on the stairs landing to his left. Down the hall to the right, he could just make out an open door. He assumed it was Tim's parents' room. For a moment, he froze and held his breath. After a few moments, he exhaled and, convinced nobody else was on the second floor, walked down the stairs.

He may as well have been an elephant crashing through a china shop. Each step seemed designed to make the most noise possible. But nobody came running down to catch him. Maybe it really was just him and Tim in the house?

All the lights downstairs were on. Glasses half full of wine and plates of partially eaten ham slices covered the tables and counters. The door in the kitchen that led to the backyard was wide open. Almost like everyone rushed out at once.

Smash!

Chris almost screamed as his heart jumped. The gentle ring of the bells had become the torrent of breaking glass.

Smash!

He tiptoed to the open door and looked outside. The backyard lights were on, casting their yellow glow up to the tree line. Beyond that was near darkness, save for the flicker here and there of what looked like firelight.

Chris thought about going back to bed. He half-turned to return inside.

"Veikleiki," the sandpaper voice spoke from the dark woods. Not loud at all, but somehow Chris heard the word clearly. An image came to his mind. He was smiling, cutting a wedding cake, and Mrs. Tennerson was there next to him.

Ding-ding.

The soothing sound of the bells returned. Chris felt his body turn and walk outside, across the backyard, and into the forest.

The backyard lights showed him the beginning of a hiking trail but didn't illuminate anything beyond that. The yellow leaves of the aspens looked like ethereal ghosts floating above him in the topaz light. He entered the darkness, hands held out in front of him. The path was straight, and he hoped that by walking forward he wouldn't run into a tree.

Smash!

A chorus of voices from further ahead, "Styrkr."

Chris continued forward. In his mind, he knew he should turn back. But something compelled him forward. Like a marionette strung along by unseen strings. His toes stubbed against a rock. He just now realized he was barefoot. Even the cold wet grass against his skin failed to snap him out of his trance. But the rock worked. He shouted out in pain and bent down to caress his foot.

A cold wind blew against his neck and made him shiver. He looked up and saw dark branches rustling overhead. The sound moved past him and towards the sound of the breaking glass ahead. Another rustling off to his right. It came to a stop near him. Then it picked up and raced forward.

It's just the wind.

Smash!

A new sound came right after. A man's screams.

Then a group of people, "*Styrkr.*"

They chanted the word just up ahead. Chris saw the flicker of torches more clearly now. They danced and bobbed between the trees.

The snapping of a branch overhead.

Something fell to the ground behind him. He heard the breathing, the wheezing, and the gasping of the thing. It couldn't' be further than a few feet away. Adrenaline took over and Chris ran forward. Hands held out in front, he blindly sprinted towards the torch light.

Whatever was behind him didn't make a sound like it was running after him. Instead, he heard the rustling of the leaves overhead. The breaking of more branches. It was getting closer.

Chris tripped and fell down a hill. He rolled over and landed in a bush. His feet felt like they were scratched all over. His back hurt. Tears welled up in his eyes and he could only think about Mom. Her smile when he brought her a homemade cupcake. He knew it wasn't good; he just poured random ingredients into a bowl and microwaved it. But Mom loved it anyway. Because she loved him. He wished for nothing more than to be home right now. It didn't matter if the town was boring or if the kids picked on him at school. He'd stomach it all if he could just be safe and at home with Mom.

He promised God then and there, lying bruised and broken in the bush, that he would be a good son from now on.

Please don't let it get me.

The branches above him cracked.

He squeezed shut his eyes and let out a whimper.

But nothing came for him. He opened his eyes and sat up straight. Wherever he had fallen, he now had a clear view of where the lights were coming from. He saw a group of men and women, maybe 20 in all. They stood in a clearing, holding lit torches. He saw Trish and her husband near the front of the group, holding hands.

Smash!

The clattering sound made its way into Chris's bones. They felt like they vibrated against his skin.

The man from before let out a howl of pain. Chris could see him now. It was Riley. He was in front of the crowd, facing the darker part of the woods. Chris's line of sight was off to Riley's left, meaning Chris could see both the man's face and the crowd.

Riley's hands and feet were spread out and tied to a wooden structure. Something made out of the aspens. The scaffolding was twisted and crudely resembled a person with arms, legs, and head. Riley's body was stretched out, matching the structure's body parts, head on head, arms on arms, feet on feet. Blood and bruises covered his flesh.

A woman stood in front of Riley. She was naked, her body covered in white and gray paint, black and red markings on her face. Her eyes were stark white and wild against her body paint. Her wild blonde hair was scattered and held in place by something that looked sticky, like sap or tar.

In her hands was a wooden mallet. It looked like the kind you could buy at any hardware store.

She cried out, "Veikleiki!"

The crowd mimicked her call.

She lifted the mallet and struck Riley's left knee. Chris saw the leg twist to the side in a way it shouldn't have been able to. Riley screamed. He was sobbing, asking her to stop.

Riley's parents pulled each other closer, smiles on their faces.

Mrs. Tennerson kissed Riley on his lips. He tried to bite her, and she backed away from him. She lifted the mallet again and swung it into his ribs. He didn't scream this time. His voice came out in muted gasps. He wheezed. The voice sounded like someone trying to breathe through a towel wrapped over their face.

Then came the sound of breaking glass. From out there in the darkness. The people shouted, "Styrkri!"

Riley was barely able to lift his head. Blood and bruises covered his flesh.

Mrs. Tennerson lifted the mallet above her head and turned to face the woods. She spun and danced wildly. The crowd of people started taking off their clothes. From somewhere on the ground they lifted up something like ashes and covered their bare bodies with it. They broke out in a frenzied maelstrom of dancing. They shrieked and howled. Fell to the ground and writhed.

Mrs. Tennerson turned back to Riley, who was still breathing, but couldn't lift his head. She helped him with that. With a swift uppercut to his jaw from the mallet. His head snapped back against the wooden edifice. Then it hung limp.

The crowd stopped moving. Mrs. Tennerson dropped the mallet. They all fell to the ground prostrate.

Chris couldn't feel anything. Not terror, not disgust. There was only a pervasive numbness filling him then. It was as if he was outside his body, floating in the treetops, looking down on the little boy hiding in the bushes.

Off in the darkness came the gentle ring of a bell. In the depths of the thick void of the forest, Chris could make out the faint image of something standing there. The light of the torches didn't touch it, but Chris could see something move just beyond the light.

It might have been dancing.

Mom's car pulled up to the house. Chris walked off the porch with his bag to meet her.

She opened the door for him, "Oh my God, honey, your eyes are so red. Did you play games all night?"

"Yeah, sorry, Mom. Let's go."

Chris got in the passenger seat and shut the door. Tim, his mom, and his dad, were standing on the porch waving at him. Tim had asked Chris to come over and play games again sometime. He said, "Sure, maybe."

Chris was sure Tim didn't know what was going on. He asked Trish that morning at breakfast where Riley was. She said he had to leave early to set something up at his new dorm. She locked eyes with Chris as she said this. A smile crept its way up her lips.

He was never coming back here. He'd be a loner for life.

Mom got in the car, shut the door, and started driving.

"Did you have fun? Trish is a doll, isn't she?"

"Yeah, sure."

"We just moved here and already she's invited me over for a special get-together next week. Apparently, the whole neighborhood gets together to send their kids off to college. Isn't that fun? Such a lovely little family vibe here. Can't wait until we get to do yours."

With all his heart and soul, Chris made himself a promise during that car ride.

Move out before finishing high school.

LONGING

I watch the man and the woman through a curtain of leaves. They're holding hands and gazing into each other's eyes. His face is all smiles and hers is all flushed cheeks. She rises on her toes and pecks his lips. He reciprocates and holds her tight in his arms.

Minutes later they are sitting on a bench. They laugh, they kiss, she pushes him away playfully. But then it all changes. Like a sudden onset of storm clouds over once tranquil waters.

I hear the words "family" and "accept." His smiles have been swallowed by a graven expression. He won't look the woman in the eyes. Tears stream down her face, giving her red eyes to match her cheeks. I hear them speak, but their words come to me like I'm underwater.

As they always do.

I think the man says, "I have to go."

I hear a "sorry" here and "don't leave" there.

Then he is rushing to his feet and walking briskly away. He doesn't look back. Her eyes stay glued to him as he nearly runs out of the park. Even after she cannot possibly see him anymore, still she stares out into the dark. As if her pleading eyes will summon the man back. The moonlight bathes the woman in silver and cold light, a feign to comfort.

Her hands bury her face behind long red nails. Her shoulders heave. I cannot hear her, but I know that she is crying.

Those hands, those red nails, they remind me of someone.

I want to go to her. To tell her it will be okay. To wipe away each tear and see that smile return to her lovely face. Everyone I see in this park is precious. I cannot bear to see their pain. All of them are so full of vibrancy, even when they think they're not. And that makes me angry. All of these lives wasted on things that don't even matter. The man who lost his job last Thursday who fed the pigeons for three hours. As if the stupid blank faces of the birds could give him guidance. The older woman just last night who wandered the paths sobbing because her husband died.

I called to her. To ease her pain. She just went on her way, oblivious to my offer.

Nobody comes to my section of the park anymore. Not since the KEEP OUT sign was nailed across the elms. Not since the weeds filled up the garden that used to be pristine. I had roses, petunias, sunflowers, and birds of paradise once. It was a palace hidden in the trees. Now all that beauty has been devoured by the wilds. Nobody visits me anymore. Nobody tends to the flowers.

Nobody lights the candles.

Night after night, I see these people with heads weighted down in despair walking by my borders.

All so stupid. What a waste. They don't understand what it means to be alive. If only they knew what it will be like when they cross over. When their bodies rot in the ground and their souls cross through that gray wall and into the empty, cold, and formless country.

I speak to them. I yell at them. I try to warn them. But nobody hears me. Nobody comes to me.

I am so *lonely.*

I scream and I groan. I strike the grass beneath with my fists. I stamp my feet. But nothing moves. Not even a blade.

I am less than a gust of wind. I am its afterthought.

Suddenly, the woman lifts her head like a startled deer and looks towards the leaves that conceal me.

This cannot be possible. Did she hear me?

Joy erupts in my heart and I start crying out to her. Oh, how good it will be to have a friend again, to have someone speak to me again, to have someone light the candles, and tend to the flowers again.

I try to push the leaves aside and show my face. My hands pass through the leaves. My hands? I can't even see them. What is happening? Why can't I push even one leaf aside? It's not fair. Cold. Numb. This nothingness I'm trapped in.

How long has it been?

What is my name?

Please, miss, can you hear me? Please hear me!

Silent words I scream. My throat would burn if I had one.

The woman starts to rise off the bench.

This is it. She's coming over. She must have heard me.

A light shines in her hand. She looks down and presses a small black object to her ear. She's talking to herself now.

Looking away from my garden.

Ignoring me.

And then she is gone. Walking down the path that will lead her out of the park.

And I am alone once again.

What is a day to me anymore? What is time? It's all one eternal moment. Drenched in paralytic agony.

I gaze out from the leaves every night, waiting for the woman to return.

Everyone else who comes at night is too preoccupied with their miserable lives to look my way. Teenagers scouring the secret places for their trysts. Drunkards falling asleep below trees well-kept.

No one sees me.

But she did. It was just once but I know that she saw me. She must have.

Yet she only came here with him. I'm so afraid she'll never come back. And then I'm lost. Lost and forgotten, buried behind this obscure wall of vegetation, sitting beneath the horned statue covered in moss. Am I afraid? Am I destitute? I do not know.

Wait, it's her. She's here! And alone. Sitting down on that bench now, directly across from my garden. She's not crying tonight. I can see the bags under her eyes. Oh, darling, you are not well. She isn't wearing makeup. Her face looks like death. If it weren't for her red nails—*so familiar*—she could pass for one of us.

Oh, I'm not completely alone, no, there are others like me. I hear their wails and their cries at night. I see the shambling ones on the paths. The ones trying to claw their way out of the soil. The ones who hang in the branches overhead.

And I hate them. I won't be like them. Alone and cold and forgotten. Ignored and unseen.

The girl is standing up now. No, she's leaving!

I scream with everything I have. A single leaf before me flutters. For just a second. Was that the wind or was that me?

She's looking in my direction now. There's fear in her tired eyes. *I'm so sorry for that. My voice can seem so sudden and intrusive to the few who have been unable to catch it.* But there's something else, I see curiosity in her arched eyebrows.

She takes a step forward. I try to leave my garden but am held back by an unseen tide.

What's your name miss? I hope your heart doesn't hurt so badly tonight.

I long for her to hear these words.

And then something happens, something I have never seen.

"My name is Lissy, who are you?"

Warmth pumps into the cavernous ice that is my chest cavity.

She spoke to me!

Me? My name is...my name is... I can't remember.

Lissy—oh, God it feels so good to know her name—she takes another step closer.

Don't scare her now.

It's okay, Lissy, your pain won't last. In a year's time you won't even remember his name. As I don't even remember mine. The expanse of time can do that to a mind, you know.

Please, won't you light the candles by my feet? They would surely warm me so.

Lissy takes one last step and she is at my border, just outside the KEEP OUT sign. She brushes the leaves and the vines aside and peers into my garden. Her pupils dilate as she stares into the darkness.

Don't be afraid Lissy, I know it's dark in here but there is nothing to be afraid of.

"Who...who are you? I hear your voice in my head."

She raises her petite pale hand, tipped in crimson paint, to her temple as if my words are splitting her head.

I'm so sorry if I'm hurting you, I don't want to. So few can hear my voice. And none as clearly as you, dear Lissy. Please, would you light my candles?

She ducks under the sign and takes a step into my garden. The wall of vines close behind her. She wades knee deep in the weeds and they rustle like ocean waves as she glides over to me. Such a lovely sound. The footsteps of a fair maiden in my garden.

She stops and lifts her hand in front of her. It's right in front of me. I reach for her hand and my own passes right through hers.

"Candles? What candles?"

The ones at my feet, don't you see them? Of course, it's too dark, of course you can't see. Look up, Lissy and see the horned statue. The candles are at its feet.

Lissy raises her dark eyes and they widen in terror.

No, no, it's okay Lissy, do not be frightened. I've been frightened for years, millennia even, time is a rushing river for me, let us be done with fear and embrace love! Ignore that heap of rock behind me.

She takes a deep breath, and I see calmness return to her face. She even smiles a little. Oh, how beautiful she is, even in the dark.

She brushes the weeds by the statute's feet aside.

"I see them. You want me to light them?"

With all my heart and soul, yes! Then we can meet face to face. And I won't be so alone here in the dark. They used to light the candles every night and I was filled with love. Back then. I can't even remember how long ago that was.

Lissy makes a move for the candles. Then a chirping sound explodes out of her pockets. She lifts that black object out and the light brightens up the garden. She speaks into that object—so silly Lissy, with these games of make believe you play—but then her face, lit up white in that light, takes a dive into fear. She looks right through me and screams. She wheels around on her heels and runs headfirst into the wall of leaves. She is gone.

My friend! The only one who hears me! Why!?

It takes me a moment and then I understand. That light must have shown her the horned statue, the darkness unveiled, covered in moss, eyes painted red. It does like to move sometimes.

It scares me too, Lissy. That's why we must light the candles so we can be rid of it! The light will dispel that damnable darkness. Please come back. Please. I can't go on anymore. I can't be so alone!

Please.

I never thought I would see Lissy again. My thoughts grew dark, well, darker than usual. I started waking up in the daylight. That's never happened to me. Oh, Lissy you are changing me! I am *becoming*.

I see a dark-haired woman walk near my border, walking with a small white dog. I think it is Lissy, but when I rush to my wall to see, I see that it was not. My Lissy is so fair, so sweet, so innocent, and her nails flash red like crimson lightning upon a pale sky.

The woman before me is ugly. I can see into her bone's marrow. Her thoughts are poison. Lissy's are the antidote.

I growl at the woman and her dog. The dog's neck hairs stand up straight and it growls back at me. The woman is too stupid to hear me. She pulls that small white thing away from me. Good thing she did, I wanted to grab it, and...and...I don't know what I wanted to do.

I scare myself now. Awake in the daylight. I thought that would cheer me up. It makes it so much worse. Seeing the happiness and the goodness that could have been mine. That should be mine. So close, yet a world away.

The horned statue is too clear in the daylight. I cannot bear to look at it.

My thoughts turn sour and rancid. If only someone would light my candles and it can all go away! And I could show them love. I could show them joy. I could show them a world without hurt.

Please.

The sun is setting. The light is draining out of the park and is being replaced by a cool, dark, pool of night. Then the impossible happens-- Lissy comes back.

She stands by the bench and stares at my garden. In one hand she has a long stick that shoots out light. In the other she holds a knife.

Why? Do you want to hurt me?

She comes closer.

"I don't know what you are, but you're in my dreams every night. Why are you torturing me? What do you want? You're driving me insane!"

Me? I am not torturing you. Am I? Am I reaching you in your dreams? I didn't know I could do that.

I must apologize, dear Lissy but I cannot hide my feelings.

The fact that she is here before me makes me want to laugh and hear my own voice dance in the air. I imagine it and it makes me glad. I can see myself dancing in this garden with my white gown twirling under the stars.

Lissy walks to my border and brushes the leaves out of the way.

She shines that light into the dark. I follow her gaze and see that light resting on the horned face. Its eyes seem somehow darker in the light. Deep set into that harsh and ridged face. The horns curve downward. They are tipped red, like Lissy's nails. The tongue curls out. It is forked.

She moves the light down and sees the knees that look like a horse's. Stone fur covers most of its lower half. She doesn't know yet about the hooved feet, I wonder what she will do when she sees them?

"I don't, I don't want to come in."

Please Lissy. Free me from him! From that grotesque statue. From his gaze and his hooves and his horns. Only you can hear me. You must light the candles and we can both be free of him.

He is evil! He keeps me here! He is the one who tortures you! Let us be free of him!

I know she believes me because she nods her head and steps forward.

"The candles are by its feet?"

By my feet, yes. No, I mean, yes, by its feet. Over here.

I try to move the weeds out of the way but my hands—do I have hands?—are useless. I am an impotent vapor dissipating before I begin.

But Lissy, no, she is flesh and blood and life and love. She alone can save me. She bends down on one knee and brushes the weeds aside. She recoils when she sees the hooves. Maybe it is the blood that cakes them which makes her hesitate. *I'm sorry you have to see this, but you must understand, things were different then. Different times and all.*

Lissy reaches into her pockets and pulls out a small yellow box. She opens it and flicks her thumb across a piece of metal.

Oh, Lissy you are showing me so many new things.

Fire! She makes fire rise out of the box. She is a goddess worthy of worship.

Wait, no, not her.

Who am I?

She lights the two candles by the hooved feet.

There is one more, behind the statue.

"Okay. And then the nightmares will stop?"

All of them, my dear. All of the heartbreaks and all of my loneliness too.

She skirts around the statue, but it is difficult for her, the weeds are nearly as tall as she is back there.

I go to help her, knowing it will be useless.

I push the grass with my hand and it bends! I look down and see my hand! Well, I see the outline of something, like a weak fog, but it is mine and it can move grass! I stamp down the grass and it bends beneath my weight.

"I have weight!"

Lissy screams.

I can speak?

"I can speak?"

The sound of my voice would bring me to tears if I had eyes.

But I do not.

Not yet at least.

Patience child. They will come.

Whose voice was that? I do not know you. Or, are you me?

It does not come again.

Lissy is cowering on the ground, her hands raised above her head like a shield.

"Lissy."

She cries out in horror.

"Lissy!"

The force of my words snap her eyes open.

"Yes?" She says.

"Just one more candle. And it is done. Then we can be together."

I see doubt color her pale face. I do not like that color on her. I like the color of her nails. Red. Wet in the dew of the grass and *red*.

I feel, not so much lonely, no, that was the wrong word this whole time.

I feel...

"There, I did it."

I wasn't even paying attention to the girl—what was her name?—but I see that the candle at the back, the one under the ratty tail of the statue, is lit.

The girl backs away from my statue and makes her way to the end of my garden. She looks so stupid to me now. The sight of her fills me with disgust. Why is she here? In my garden? How dare she.

"Oh, is that you? I thought, I thought you would be something scary." The girl laughs. The sound grates against my ears. What is she talking about?

I look at my hands. White as the moon with red nails. Growing longer. Sharper.

I feel my hair. Long and raven black. I am beautiful. I am lovely. I am to be adored. My garden is to be kept lit. The weeds are to be cut. The statue is to be at bay by the fire's light. I am to be loved.

I am a queen.

I am love.

I am...so hungry.

The girl smiles as she approaches me. She must trust me now.

"Is this when my pain goes away?" She asks insipidly.

"Yes, child, this is the end."

I open my long arms, so long and so wide they fill the garden, and embrace her. She embraces me. I feel her sobs as her chest convulses against my own.

I feel her heartbeat connect with my own.

I love you, you stupid little thing. And I am sorry.

I remember now. I haven't been truly awake for over a hundred years. And I am *hungry*.

I feel my teeth grow long and sharp. I push the woman away from me and hold onto her shoulders with incredible strength. Oh, how I have forgotten my strength!

She was smiling as her face was buried in my bosom. She wipes the tears out of her eyes. Then she looks up. And sees me. Truly sees me.

She screams and struggles. She thrashes against my cold iron grip.

Oh, how I have missed this.

There is no one to offer her to me with song and dance. I must take her on my own.

Oh, well.

I sink my teeth into her neck. I am able to close my jaw fully as I bite into her. I drink from her life. I feel her joy and her pain and her love and her regret flow into me. I feel the pain when Mark left her. Married to another woman? How dare he? I shall visit him soon as well.

I bite down again, harder this time, until her head is no longer attached to her pretty neck. Her tiny head falls into the weeds with a *thud*. I bite down harder on the part left exposed between her shoulders. I bury my face into her as she did into me.

This is love.

The more I take from her the more solid I feel. The girl loves me. She has given me her everything.

Thank you.

I have my fill. And when I am done I am satisfied and I am happy and I am alive.

For a moment.

And then I realize how hungry I am again.

So soon.

Always hungry.

I walk over to my border of leaves and watch them wither before my touch and turn to ash. The vines flee before my presence. I break the KEEP OUT sign under my foot.

I walk through that border and into the park.

Oh, look, look at how surprised the woman with the dog is now. The dog runs from her and leaves her shaking before me.

"Now you see me?"

I smile.

I tower over her.

So good to be alive.

FRIED RICE

I know you all like reading this blog for my usual monster movie deep dives. So, forgive me for assuming this, but this might be of interest to you.

She was there again tonight.

Some of you might remember that I wrote a little bit about her last time.

She's always at the same convenience store, the one right outside my apartment block. I used to love that place. It was the perfect spot to run and grab a coffee on the way to the office, or a cheap dinner on my way back. Sato usually keeps me until ten every night—literally doing nothing—so that store is the only way I get my dinner before hitting the bed and waking up at five the next day.

That store (not going to name it out of respect for the owners) has the best microwavable fried rice ever, even better than my mother's. Sorry, but I have to speak the truth.

This woman, I've been seeing her there for about two months now. An elderly woman dressed in a brown lace shawl thrown over her head and shoulders and a black skirt that nearly touches the floor. She's bent forward like she spent her whole life farming. Kind of like a bunch of old folks we have back home. I didn't really think much about her the first few times I went in. Wouldn't have thought about her at all if she wasn't blocking my way to the frozen fried rice bags.

The first time wasn't a big deal. Her tiny frame was practically glued to the refrigerated shelf and there was no way I could get to the rice without disturbing her. So, I let it slide and didn't try to bother her. A few more times after that, I went in and didn't even want the rice. But I did notice her. Tilted forward, back bent, like she was praying at the altar of fried goods. Once I timed her out of curiosity. I stood there for ten minutes watching her and she didn't move. I gave up, well, because I was being the odd one just gawking at this woman.

The store has other good things. Rice balls with salmon filling, frozen yogurt, that beer I like—you know the one, and even steam buns filled with pizza ingredients. I could have been satisfied with those; I should have been satisfied with those. Then maybe none of this would have happened.

But recently Sato's got us going into hyperdrive for a new product launch next month, so it's even more overtime on top of what we were already doing. I've been getting home at eleven and I'm so damn tired I can't even think straight anymore.

All that to say, I really, really want some fried rice. Like, nothing else will do. It's like a part of me is craving a slice of home and this is the closest I can get to it. Sure, I could always go somewhere else to grab some. But that would require me to go out of my way to a different store, and I just don't have the energy.

And tonight, I was craving it so bad I could kill someone for it. Not literally, but you know what I mean.

I ran into the store and for a moment it looks like she's not there. The shelf with the rice on it is around the corner from the checkout counter and usually I see a part of her black skirt swaying out, letting me know she was there. Tonight, I saw nothing.

My heart nearly exploded in joy. I could nearly taste the oily rice, with that slight taste of sweetness mixed with saltiness. My mouth was watering as I rounded the corner. I probably looked like a deranged weirdo to the guy on duty. But when I turned down the aisle, my heart dropped.

There she was. There she *always* is.

My joy turned to irritation, borderline rage. I approached her, closer than I'd ever gotten to her before. I mean, being old doesn't entitle you to make other people's lives harder, does it? The first thing that hit me was the smell. A heavy perfume seemed to be seeping from her dwarfish stature. It was like vanilla, but so thick I coughed and gagged on its fumes. And there was something under that smell, hiding under it. It was both a sweet and a rancid meat smell. Like the time I left a steak under the couch by mistake and found it a week later.

I hesitated. It wasn't that I was scared, I felt sorry for her. She probably hadn't bathed in weeks and was masking her stench with the perfume. I imagined her life; no family or friends to come calling, no one noticing her gradual descent to the grave.

I cleared my throat.

"Excuse me."

She responded by leaning her skeletal frame to the right. But not enough for me to go in and grab the rice.

"Excuse me, ma'am. I just need to grab something, if you could..."

The woman leaned back to the left. Her face was pointed down and was shrouded by her shawl. Come to think of it, out of all the times I've run into her, I've never seen her face.

I spoke to her once more, and still no response.

As much as I wanted the rice, I decided to not make a big deal out of the situation.

I resigned myself to the corn dogs instead.

Two weeks since I last wrote down my thoughts about the strange woman at the store. I stopped by the store a few times to grab other things and, sure enough, she was still there. Rocking side to side, face staring at the floor, like she was a part of the infrastructure of the place more than a real person. Just a thing, like a door swinging on its hinges.

Tonight, the craving was so strong for the fried rice. I made up my mind on the train home that I was just going to grab it even if she wouldn't move out of the way. I wasn't going to touch her or push her or anything. But I would have to get really close to her.

I thought of the smell as I walked into the store. My skin crawled and I shivered, even though it was hot and humid out. The man at the counter, a young boy in his teens, really, made the briefest eye contact with me. Funny, out of all the nights I encountered this woman and can recall all the details about her, I never really paid attention to the staff. This kid might have been the regular guy on shift, I don't know. But when our eyes met, I saw apprehension in him.

At first, I thought he felt the same way I did. That he too was horrified by the munchkin woman who smelled like raw sewage. But later on, my way home I thought about it more. Maybe it was me that he was scared of.

Anyway, I pass the kid at the counter and turn down the aisle. And wouldn't you know it, there she is. Big fat surprise. I can taste that rice once again. I can smell the oil wafting up into the air. It's not about good food, you know, it's about the memories and the feelings that it evokes. I needed to touch base with home, with a reality that was kinder and more human than these soulless nights in Tokyo. I guess I just miss home.

Sorry, I'm sounding like a madman. It's just so hard to express what has happened.

So, yeah, back to tonight. I had made up my mind to confront this lady.

I imagined myself saying, "Who do you think you are? There are people here who should be able to get what they pay for. Why don't they matter, huh?"

But as I drew nearer, her pungency almost made me throw up.

I thought about going back home. I had no spine to grab the rice. But one other thing bothered me to no end.

Her face. I still hadn't seen her face. Maybe if I could make some eye contact with her, it'd be easier to get her attention. Maybe she was a kind old woman who just had some mental decline. I was sure if I could look her in the eyes, I could set things straight between us.

Not that she knew I was there, anyway, so I guess I could set things right in my own mind.

Anyway, I got closer to her. Maybe about an arm's length away. The smell was so powerful it felt like I was swimming in a pool. Like the air itself was thick with the miasma to the point where physical objects had to push to get through.

I said, "Excuse me, ma'am?"

I bowed and smiled. She ignored me.

I bent down lower, almost as low as she was, to try and get a glimpse of her face. But it was just barely out of sight. Her shawl covered some of it and she seemed to be purposefully looking away from me. I would have had to sit on the floor to get a good look at her.

I spoke to her two more times and tried to duck my head under hers to get a look. I know I must have looked insane to anyone in the store at the moment, but there was only the boy at the counter.

This woman. This fucking woman. She wouldn't meet my eyes. She was doing it on purpose. Playing with me. She knew I just wanted some damn rice and all she had to do was lean to the side a bit more, just a few inches. Is that so much to ask for?

You're probably asking why I didn't just put my hand in front of her face and take the rice.

Because, to do that, my hand would have had to touch her forehead. That's how close she was to the rice! I'm not going to touch somebody like that and get arrested and lose my job. No, I'm a respectable person. I'm a good man. I am doing my best and I just want one thing. I can handle the overtime, I can handle Sato breathing down my neck, his breath smelling like mints just barely covering the tobacco scent, I can handle the one-room apartment the size of a broom closet.

I can take all of that if I can just have some fucking fried rice.

I did something tonight.

It's hard to put into words exactly what happened. My hand hurts as I write this. The knuckles and joints keep locking up like I have arthritis or something. And I'm just so cold. But I need to get this out.

I touched her. I saw her. And I'm afraid this was the biggest mistake of my life.

I had the day off today. So, I did what I do every weekend and I slept until two in the afternoon. I slumped around the apartment in my underwear, foraging for potato chips in my cupboards and watching prank videos on YouTube. I had no intention of leaving the apartment until I woke up from my second nap.

I had this dream that the woman was eating my rice. Right in front of me. She was taking clumps of it out of a pot on the floor with her bare hands. She looked me in the eye and laughed, no, *cackled* at me. She shoved the food into her withered mouth. I could see black teeth in that tiny hole and peach fuzz like mold on her chin. She ate with her mouth open and made these awful smacking sounds. She mushed the rice up in her mouth and I could see it sticking to her dead teeth and sticking bits stringing between her tongue and the roof of her mouth.

I couldn't do anything but sink into the floor. I grew smaller, like a child. She rushed me. Shoved that rice into my mouth. I woke up on my kitchen floor gasping for breath.

More than air, my body craved that rice. Every fiber of my being screamed out for that rice. I nearly ran out of the apartment mostly naked; the craving was so strong. So I got dressed, didn't even bother washing my face or combing my hair.

I know I must have looked like a wild man. Bloodshot eyes. No shower for the day. I realized as I left my apartment building that I had some brown stains on the front of my white shirt. I must have just taken something from the dirty clothes pile on the bathroom floor and put it on.

I know what I looked like to him. The boy at the counter. And I know that I must have been muttering something and maybe even twitching a bit. I was just too hungry to give a shit. I wouldn't have been surprised if he called the police on me. I didn't do anything wrong, but I must have looked like I was about to because he cringed and cowered behind that counter when I walked in. I smiled at him, but he only winced at me like I was going to hit him.

No, I've never hit anyone before. I'm a good man. I don't cause trouble.

I turned the corner and there she was.

I started laughing and muttering to myself. I don't remember what I said. And if I'm aware of how crazy it must have looked, that means I'm not crazy, right?

I stomped my way over to the woman. Her shield of rotten stench wasn't going to stop me this time. Nor was her leaning away from me going to keep me from seeing her face. Least of all, I was getting that rice no matter what I would have to do.

"Excuse me, ma'am," I nearly yelled at her.

Still nothing from her. She was taunting me. Using her age and her diminutiveness to make me feel bad. But no, not tonight. Tonight, I was getting what I came for.

"If you don't talk to me, I'll have to move you."

Still nothing.

So, I did it. I made the move. I made the biggest mistake of my life.

I stepped right next to her, holding my breath to save myself from her smell. I leaned into her with my right shoulder. Softly! I'm not a monster.

I started to push her out of the way and butt my way in front of her. I expected some resistance, but she moved out of the way like she was made out of cardboard.

And then there it was. Looking right at me. The rice. One whole frozen bag of rice, all for me, and only me.

I grabbed the bag. It was cold to the touch, but I felt another freezing sensation on my right elbow. Colder than the bag.

I looked to my right and I saw a hand, if you could call it that. It was so small, like a child's, but covered with liver spots. So wrinkled, it looked like broken-in leather. And it was as cold as ice. Then the pain started.

Like I just jumped into an ice bath at the bathhouse. The shock of the ice went up my arm and into my fingers. Then she gripped my arm tighter. It felt like tiny teeth were biting my flesh.

"What are you doing!?" I cried.

I turned to face her. I regret that I did. It would have been better for her to just take my arm without me ever looking at her. I saw her face. No longer was she bent over; she was standing tall. She couldn't have been any taller in reality, but she seemed like she was much taller than me, even.

And her face.

This is hard to write.

She had none.

I mean, she didn't have a face! The skeletal structure for a nose and eyes and a mouth was there but she didn't have a nose or eyes or a mouth. It was like someone took old saggy skin and stretched it over a mannequin. It looked like she was speaking, because I could see something moving, under the skin, where her mouth should have been.

I screamed and fell backwards to the ground. The boy came running over, holding a mop handle like it was a weapon.

"Look! She's a monster!" I cried.

But when I turned my eyes back to the woman, she was gone.

"Who?" the boy asked.

"The... the woman. The one that's always here. She's always bent over the fried rice, in a shawl!"

"Mister, I've been seeing you come in a lot lately and stare at this spot. But I've never seen a woman like that."

I went over to where she was, but she was gone. Did anyone but me ever see her? I should have been terrified. I should have run out of there screaming. But you know what I did instead? Seeing how I had unbarred access, I picked up the bag of fried rice and came home.

I almost cried; I was so happy. Just to make sure, I even ran back in right after buying them, just to see if she was there, and she wasn't!

But none of that matters now. I can't eat the rice. I came home, heated it all up in my microwave, and sat down to eat. My right arm was killing me. I lifted the sleeve and saw a deep purple bruise extending from my elbow to my wrist. And it was cold to the touch. I shrugged it off and plunged my spoon into the steaming bowl of rice. My mouth was watering. I lifted the rice to my face and tried to put it in my mouth.

I say tried, because there was no opening where my mouth should have been. I stabbed the skin with the spoon as I tried to shovel in another spoonful. It was like skin had grown over my mouth. I ran to the bathroom mirror and looked at myself.

No mouth.

Isn't it funny? I still have my eyes, for now. But my mouth, the one thing that would allow me to enjoy what my soul has been yearning for.

Gone.

My skin is sagging too. The ice feeling is spreading to my chest now.

And there's another craving rising up in me.

Cigarettes? I've never smoked before – why would I like that? And I feel like I know where to find some, several blocks over at a different store.

But this feeling, not to smoke them. I just... I just want to look at some of them for a while.

Come to think of it, I think they're the kind Sato smokes.

FOUNDATIONS

The windows shattered and rained down its broken pieces in a torrent of shards. The tables shook and the people screamed as the lights went out. A display case of mugs and coffee beans fell over. The display case covering the baked goods shattered. A teenage boy tripped over a table and sent all the drinks and food flying.

Pat dove under a table and covered his head as the impromptu shelter shook violently. A light fell and broke apart on the floor a few feet away from him.

The quaking stopped.

Car alarms replaced the sound of the deep rumbling that had come from underground. Pat heard someone crying nearby. Everything was dark aside from the firefly glow of the smartphones lighting up around him.

In the last three months since moving to Tokyo, this was by far the worse earthquake he had experienced, or even thought possible of experiencing.

He checked his phone and saw the last message he sent before the quake struck: IF THAT'S HOW YOU FEEL ABOUT IT, WHATEVER!!

Sara hadn't read it yet. He tried calling her, but his phone had no signal. A few of the other customers were now standing so Pat thought it was safe to do the same. He pulled himself up on a booth seat and stood with shaking knees.

A man and woman stood near him, bent over scrolling through their phones. Pat could see that they, too, were having connection issues.

"Excuse me, do you speak English?"

The man looked up at him with wide eyes, highlighted by a deathly blue glow of his phone. "Little," he said as he gestured a pinch with his fingers.

"Was that normal?"

"No, no normal." The man tried to summon another word from deep inside but gave up. "Sorry," he apologized as the woman pulled his arm and led him away.

Pat left the ruined café. It was slightly brighter outside; some of the streetlights and building lights were still working, though most were dead. Thousands of people flooded the streets of Shibuya. Pat could see multiple people on the ground, not moving. He jumped over a crack that had formed in the sidewalk. He passed by a few cars that were overturned on their sides. Water sprayed him from a fire hydrant that shot a spray of water into the air.

The people were alive with the insect buzz of gossip. Some were yelling into their phones, others tried to climb up on park benches to get reception.

Is everyone's phone dead?

Pat checked his again and looked at the message he sent Sara. His anger had evaporated the moment the earth turned into jelly. Looking out at the destruction of the city filled him with a new emotion: panic. Sara might be out there and in trouble. Pat looked to his right at a small gathering of people trying to lift a fallen streetlight off an older man. Blood poured from his head and his feet twitched.

He imagined her in the same situation.

Pat started moving down the sidewalk to get away from the crowds, which were now growing so large he feared he wouldn't be able to move through them soon. He turned down a side street that he knew led to a quieter neighborhood. He had taken it dozens of times in the past few weeks to get to Sara's apartment from the station. A fire was consuming the karaoke place to his left. People were climbing out the second story window and dropping down below. He couldn't see if they landed safely.

The ground shook.

He felt the vibration in his feet, not more than a tremor, almost like he was walking across a heavily trafficked bridge. Someone in the crowd must have noticed it too and started screaming. A dozen people took flight and Pat's shoulder was clipped by someone. He fell to the ground on his back. Not hurt. But when he tried to stand, he was pushed from behind. A young woman had fallen over him. Somebody else over her. Pat's breathing became shallow and rapid. He tried to claw his way back to his feet but was unable to get out from under the woman. A man ran by and stepped on the woman's stomach, crushing Pat into the ground even more. He could barely breathe. She cried out in horror. Pat finally pulled himself out from under her and stood up.

He looked down at the woman and saw her roll up into a ball. For a moment he thought about helping her until more people rushed by like a river of human flesh and then he could see her no more. He was pushed to the side, his back up against a stone wall. Maybe a hundred people flew past him in just a few seconds until they, too, came to a standstill. Pat was a tall man and could see over the heads of most of the crowd. Thousands deep by now. There was no empty space on the street to run to.

Pat was shoved harder into the wall. It was a cool Autumn night when he left the apartment. Now, in the midst of all these people, sweat washed over his face. He reached his arms above his head to grasp something, anything that could save him. His hands touched cool metal. He gripped whatever it was and pulled himself up. It took a few moments to wrench his legs free from the crush of the people. He used the shoulder of someone to help lift himself up. He turned around and threw himself at the fire escape. He clambered up and gasped for breath in the relative safety he had found.

He looked out over the crowd. Thousands of bobbing heads. He knew they were all individual people, but all he could see was a mass, indistinct from one another, an unfeeling stream of humanity.

A deep rumble shook the fire escape and Pat clung to the stairs. The metal bashed against the side of the wall and nearly shook him off. The roar of the crowds rose into an unbearable cry of desperation. He found himself incapable of uttering a sound. All the remaining lights on the street went out. Pat saw lights from phones flash here and there. The karaoke's flames provided some light off in the distance. But the space around them was thick with darkness. A deep and impenetrable black curtain that felt wholly unnatural.

A sound like roaring fire or maybe a train screaming down the tracks came from somewhere beneath him. A black mist swallowed the fire in the karaoke place and the silver lights of the phones. The people screamed in the darkness. The building Pat clung to rattled like a house of sticks. A thundering *BOOM* erupted from the street.

More screaming. Most of the voices growing faint as if they were traveling a great distance in a matter of seconds. Pat heard loud thuds and wet ripping sounds. Terror in every voice.

Then it was silent.

Not a single voice graced the air.

The shaking stopped.

Pat could feel his heartbeat in his throat and his fingertips went numb.

Thousands of screams. Thousands of people. In an instant reduced to absolute silence. The darkness ebbed in front of Pat like a moving wall. Like the pit of an endless abyss. He almost thought he could see something moving in that black canvas. Something big. He wanted to yell out and hear a voice return to him from the void, but the words refused to escape his lips.

A rush of wind blew against him. Warm and humid. It blew his hair back. Reeking of damp moss and rot. It sounded like a snort. The kind a large animal like a cow or a horse would make. Pat felt the urge to piss himself. He was frozen with fear.

Another *boom* and the building shook. Then it settled down. A minute later the thunder came again, from further down the street, but still strong enough to shake the fire escape. Pat counted the booms like his Mom taught him to do with thunder storms.

What was it, every second meant it was a mile away right?

He counted until the next sound, further away, by a whole two seconds.

But who was he kidding? This wasn't thunder. It sounded like...like footsteps.

Impossible.

They carried off further away until the shaking stopped, and the sounds faded in intensity. But they were still there. Like fireworks going off across a valley, they never fully left.

Pat leaned over the railing and looked down. Too dark. Like the world had been doused in oil. It gave him the sensation of floating in space, of being rootless, no reference points, a world beyond sense.

"H-hello?"

He should have kept quiet.

No sooner had he spoken than *it* had responded. From down there on the street, if the street was still there. A deep wail rose up from the ground like an offering to an absent god. The volume of the cry made Pat's heart skip a beat and it popped his ears. The sensation soon turned to pain as his eardrums ruptured. The pain spiked and nearly made him sob until it quickly passed.

Then came the red. The light—if he could call it that, it was thick and almost fog-like-- burned from the street. No, from beneath it. In the crimson glow that was growing stronger, Pat could see that the street itself was mostly gone. In its stead a deep chasm. He imagined the crowd of people, all of them with plans for tomorrow and loved ones at home, now swallowed into the earth. Beside the hole he saw body parts. Arms. Legs. Half a torso. All scattered about the little that remained of the street.

The scarlet glow washed over his face and he could feel the heat that it emitted. And there was something, moving down there. Deep below. Some dark shape, made darker still when contrasted with the light. It was getting bigger. Coming closer. Escaping the hole.

Did it hear me?

Pat looked around for some way off the fire escape, somewhere that wasn't down *there*. The stairs of the fire escape were behind him. He ran up them until the stairs ended in a ladder. He jumped on it and feverishly climbed up its rungs. It shook as he went up a full story. The metal clanged and rattled noisily. Pat feared it would alert what was down there to his presence. He made it to a door and tried the handle.

Locked.

He looked down and saw the dark thing, even bigger than it was seconds ago, almost to the top of the chasm. Pat climbed higher, to the next floor. He made it a few feet below another door. He could see that it was slightly open. The only problem was the ladder had separated from the wall and leaned out and away from the building. There was no climbing higher.

Pat maneuvered around the twisted metal and placed his feet on the uppermost rung possible and crouched, balancing his body on the ladder. The next landing was a few feet away, above him. he would have to jump up, grab the ledge, and pull himself up. His feet caused the ladder to shake like a reed in the wind. The wailing grew louder. Off in the distance he heard the thundering. It was getting louder. Closer.

He jumped. His hands grasped the landing. And slipped. He fell backward and his ass hit the part of the ladder that was leaning away from the wall. Causing the whole thing to fall. He laid back against the ladder as it slowly bent down towards the ground. His back was facing the street so he had to brace himself against the falling ladder awkwardly. He felt gravity shift and he was soon upside down. The ladder didn't crash to the ground, the landing was soft and slow. In the inky dark Pat could see the asphalt just beneath him. He rolled backwards off the ladder and tumbled onto the street. In front of him was the chasm, spewing out its red light. It was all he could see in the dark. Something moved right at the edge of the opening of the hole. The wailing exploded out of the crack. It sounded like the thing was right at the opening, about to come up and into the street.

Pat turned around, fumbled for his phone in his pocket, and took it out. His mind registered the new message from Sara but he had more pressing concerns at the moment. He turned on the flashlight. The dark was so thick the light only revealed two or three feet in front of him.

He could see that it wasn't just the absence of light, the darkness was *something*. The light dispelled some of it, but he could see the black mist floating around like dust or fog. Like the very shadows had come alive.

He walked forward, too afraid to run into the unknown. He tripped over a slab of cement but caught his balance. The street rumbled with the approaching thunder of what he thought were footsteps. The remaining cars on the sidewalk bounced and shook with each step. The blast of warm wind hit the back of his neck. He heard a scraping of something sharp against the cement behind him. He imagined it coming from the thing in the hole, now on the street.

He ran.

He could tell he was on the street, bisected as it was by the crack. The walls of the buildings to his left were fractured and leaning forward, about to fall. A sudden drop and a deep river of red was to his right. He leaped over debris and scooters and bikes. The darkness rushed at him like he was driving too fast on a dark mountain road. A body appeared before him. No time to stop. The shaking and the booming was right there. Right behind him. He briefly noted the absence of eyes in the dust caked face as he ran by it. A pile of wreckage, the remnants of a building, sprang up in front of him, blocking his path forward.

More bodies. On the ground. In pieces. Some leaning halfway out of broken windows. Even one strewn over a still standing streetlight.

Shaking. Booming. Thundering.

He turned left and saw a gap in the building at its base from where it broke in two, lit up by flashing red emergency lights. Inside he could see a hallway and on the other side of it an open door to the next street over. He ran inside and across the hall. He almost went through the door and into the next street, but it was swallowed in absolute darkness. He'd be vulnerable if he was out on the streets. He wondered how long the building would stay standing before it completely collapsed.

Screeching metal and then a crash. He looked back at the street he was just on and saw a car fly across the gap in the wall before it crashed into something. He backed up and into a part of the building not exposed to the outside. He ducked down behind an arcade game tilted on its side. The pulsing red lights washing over the room worked in tandem with a beeping sound from an alarm.

The whole room shook.

He heard a man yelling something from the street he was about to run into. A woman responded to him. Their voices, unintelligible to Pat, were laden with panic.

The roof caved in. A section of the ceiling came crashing down on top of the arcade machine and missed crushing Pat. Dust shot up like the plume of a volcanic eruption. He saw *something*, large and dark, coming in from the fallen ceiling. It rose out of the debris and moved towards the other street. The man and woman screamed. Pat heard wet *thwocks* sounds and they both went silent.

Twenty minutes passed before Pat dared to move again. The thundering had passed maybe seven minutes ago, but he could still hear it, faint and distant.

It wouldn't be true to say that Pat's life flashed before his eyes while he ran for his life into the arcade but rather his regrets. Sara was pregnant. He wanted to keep the kid; she wanted to go back to America and raise it herself. Said he wasn't the responsible type. Pat took out the phone and looked at Sara's message. That action alone took him the full twenty minutes. So paralyzed by fear was he, so afraid to make a sound as simple as reaching into his pockets.

Sara's message: *What's going on? My calls can't get through to you. I'm at home. It's so dark and there's something happening, I'm hearing this awful sound, like, I don't know, something in the ground, screaming. And there's something in the building, it's eating people's eyes! The fuck am I saying. But I saw it through the keyhole! Please help me.*

Sent nearly half an hour ago. No other messages. Five missed calls. He dialed her number. No sound was on the line. He tried sending a text but nothing. Pat crawled out from under the machine and looked around. He knew this place. It was the arcade around the corner from the Starbucks he liked going to. Which meant that Sara's place should be a five-minute walk out the door. The one he heard the screaming of that man and woman come from.

The flashing red light and the beeping spoke of something to come. He felt like he was in a plane, about to leap off into a storm, hoping that his chute would open in time. He walked over to the open door. Somehow not covered in the debris from whatever had come crashing through the roof.

More people screaming. He could hear them out there, just barely. And then they went silent. Islands of human suffering rising up and going out here and there. He hoped his turn wasn't next. The inhuman wailing was there too. The cry of that thing he saw in the chasm. And the thundering footsteps. All of this was far off, or so he judged. This might be his best time to move. Or he could stay where he was and hope it would all pass him by.

He looked at the message again. He thought of Sara. The last time they met, just over an hour ago, they were at the café, the same one he was at when the shaking began. She wanted to move back to America, he wanted to stay in Japan, and he blew up on her.

Sara was alone now. In the dark. And something was outside her door.

Eating people's eyes?

All he wanted was to see her again. Safe and well. Immense shame filled his chest.

He laughed at himself. No matter how big that fight seemed then, now in light of his current situation, it was nothing.

He switched his phone's light on and walked out into the darkness. Howls pierced his ears from somewhere above him, maybe from the rooftops that were beyond his sight. The constant rhythm of vibrating earth shot through his feet. Sara's place was up a hill, second street on the right from the arcade. Which would mean he'd have to turn left onto the street from where he was now. Assuming the corner he stood on was the correct one.

Pat walked down the street slowly, watching his feet for holes, for bodies. There was no chasm on this street, but the road was broken up, looking like a frozen still of a turbulent ocean. There were no bodies here. How could that be? There must have been thousands of people on every street. And if they met the same end as the mutilated corpses he saw earlier, then where were the bodies now?

He passed two streets, keeping his hand running alongside the buildings for guidance like a blind man, and turned onto the one with a hill. The black air grew thicker. Not like smoke. It felt like he was moving through water, not strong enough to give his body resistance, but enough to let him know it was there. He involuntarily tasted it on his tongue. Chalky and dry like ash but also sweet. He wiped the greasy feeling off his face and looked at his palm. It was as black as if he had picked up charcoal.

He continued on up the hill. Before he arrived at Sara's apartment, he was struck by that wet *thwock* sound again. He heard someone make a gurgling sound. Pat bent down behind an upturned piece of asphalt and shut off his light. He peered out into the dark in the direction of the sound but could see nothing. He heard a scuffling of something sharp scratching against the road.

"*Iyada!*" He heard a woman scream.

A flash of light that must have been her phone. It shook and bounced chaotically. The white light revealed something that shocked the blood in his veins into instant ice. Long limbs like a spider. Taller than a streetlight. Writhing hairs or tentacles on its dark skin. In a lightning quick motion, he saw one of the spindly limbs strike out towards the light. The woman screamed and the sound was abruptly cut short and with it the light. Then came the *thwock*, another gurgle, and the sound of something heavy hitting the ground like a sack of sand. A scuttling sound of many sharp appendages traveled up above him until it was gone.

He almost wished he had seen nothing.

What the fuck was that?

Whatever it was killed that woman. And it did not shake the earth as it walked. What he had seen was too small to have made those earth-shaking sounds.

Bigger ones out there.

But what made that wailing sound?

He got up and ran forward. In that woman's brief lighting up of the street he had seen no large obstructions on the road. He sprinted hard until he reached the front doors of Sara's building. The glass doors were shattered and tilted to the side, as was the whole building. Aside from his phone's light, Pat went in absolute darkness and came to the stairwell. He paused to listen and heard nothing.

He made his way up the stairs, one step at a time, pausing to listen. His terror growing and his heartbeat so loud it was hard to hear what could be there. He made it to the third floor; Sara was on the fifth. He could see cracks in the wall and the occasional split in a step, but overall, the stairwell was in good condition.

A groaning sound of metal grinding on metal came from somewhere on the first floor. The building shook slightly. He heard something crash overhead in one of the apartments. He covered his light with his palm and waited. No more sounds.

He walked up the rest of the stairs and came to the fifth floor. He pushed at the steel door, but it refused to budge fully open. Just enough for him to squeeze his body through. A blinking yellow emergency light illuminated the tilted hallway. He walked past room 501 on his right and heard someone sobbing inside. Sara was down the hall in room 507.

Sorry, I have to go.

Deep gash marks were on the doors of rooms 502 and 503. The same incisions were on the walls and the ceiling, like something large had barged its way down the hall. In the flashing lights he could see red streaks on the floor. The door to room 504 was missing, torn off its hinges. He crept by it just in case one of *them* was inside. He made it past the room without hearing anything unusual. 505 and 506 looked untouched by the chaos.

507.

Pat's heart fell to his feet. The door was split in two down the middle. He held his breath without even realizing it. He squeezed between the two halves of the door and entered the room. The lights from the hall splashed into the dark pit of the apartment. His phone revealed little spotlights of what used to be Sara's life. A vase of purple flowers on the kitchen counter, somehow still standing. The T.V., lying face down on the living room floor. The broken window in the living room. Around the jagged shards of glass, he saw red. Painted over both the remaining glass and the wall surrounding it.

He walked over to the window, holding his hand over his mouth, fighting back tears.

"Sara?"

He felt inside his pocket. It was somehow still there. The cheap engagement ring. He never got around to proposing to her at the café, he lacked the nerve.

Pat went from room to room and didn't find her. He returned to the broken window and looked out it. Nothing but a sheer straight drop down to the street.

"Shit!"

He recoiled from the window. Red light exploded off in the distance, like a flash of lightning, over by where the arcade was. The crimson light revealed something that nearly broke his mind. The light died down. It was only for the briefest few seconds that he saw it. Something taller than the buildings, some of them eight stories high. He saw a faceless figure hunched over the cityscape. Long arms that touched the ground. What could have been a hood or a curtain of flesh draped over its form. Just as the light died down it turned towards the apartment.

Then darkness once more.

Boom. Boom. Boom.

The footsteps had returned. Coming towards the apartment from the direction of the arcade.

It couldn't have seen me!

The room shook. The flower vase fell to the ground with a smash.

The red light flashed again. He saw it rise from chasms in the ground just outside the apartment. It lit up the silhouette of the towering thing.

Now he could see the gaping hole where a face should have been. It wailed and screamed.

Pat turned and ran out into the hall. And froze. In the blinking lights he saw one of the smaller spider things in the hall, ripping into room 501. It shoved its large body into the doorway in a move that should have been impossible given its size. The person inside the room screamed. Then came the *thwock* as their body was flung out into the hall and crashed into the opposing wall.

Lifeless. Eyeless.

He saw a crab-like appendage emerge from the room and drag the body back inside.

The building shook harder. He felt his body tilting. Then he noticed a soccer ball in the hall rolling.

Wailing. A cry of pain and longing. It shook his rib cage with its intensity.

He looked behind him and into Sara's room.

Another flash of red. In that glow he saw the endless void of the faceless thing. He saw the black hole that was its mouth and the stars that were its teeth.

Then he was rolling down the hall. His body tumbled and flew down the stairwell.

The rest of the building came down to join him.

THE WHITE FEATHER CLUB

I t all started with an eye in the wall.

Not any normal, white eyeball, with a bit of color in the iris and attached to the head of a decent, law-abiding citizen. This eye was stained piss-yellow with specs of black floating around its surface. And it was wide open. Staring. Unblinking. It should have been dry due to the exposure, but it glistened wet in the light.

Mie found the eye after she got out of the bath one day after work. Normally, she would stumble around the apartment like the undead at this time, barely awake to the details around her, burdened by the stress of caring for other people's children all day. As the steam from the tub soaked into the grimy walls and faded away, she noticed the hole in the wall just to the left of her mirror. It wasn't there yesterday, was it? For weeks, she could have sworn she heard scratching from within the walls but had been too scared to check it out. A mouse or rat or even a nest of cockroaches could be living in her tiny apartment walls, and uncovering that truth was worse than pretending it didn't exist.

But this she couldn't ignore. Not when the lidless and jaundiced eye was boring a hole into her own from inside that opening. She screamed and ran out of the bathroom when she saw the eye. Promptly called the police and they showed up twenty minutes later. The cops found her outside her front door, dressed normally but hair still soaking wet; she told them she couldn't go back inside with the eye, as if it could see her no matter where she was inside.

Mie's apartment, number 105, shared a wall, the unfortunate wall the eye was stuck in, with apartment 104. Police pounded on that door, but no one answered. Having reasonable suspicion to act on, they got the key from the building manager and stepped inside.

There was no noticeable smell, they said, because the body hadn't been dead for longer than just a few hours. The tenant, one Sota Kobayashi, was found glued to the inside of his bathroom wall by an unknown adhesive. Broken pieces of plaster and wood were scattered about the entry point to the wall, but his naked body was found three feet away from the hole, sandwiched inside, suggesting he had crawled his way to the spot. Police say the man used a hammer to both break into the wall and make the hole. His arms were found stretched over his head and his face was stiffened into an eternal smile frozen in time. His right eye was wedged in the hole. Splinters were found stuck in the sides of the eye, causing officers to question whether the man was aware of the pain or not while he spied on his neighbor.

Cause of death was unknown, but they ruled out homicide. No next of kin.

Mie learned most of these details weeks later, after requesting them at the precinct. Exactly one week after something far more traumatic than the yellow eye came creeping into her life. But it wasn't the nature of Sota's death that she was interested in. He could burn in hell for all she cared. What she wanted to know was if he had a tattoo of a nine-headed snake on his back.

He did.

"Mie, what are you doing? You let him get away without upselling him! When he comes back from the restroom, get him to buy *something* at least."

Yuna stared down at Mie, arms crossed over her silver dress, eyes burning with disdain. At least they weren't yellow.

"I'm sorry, I'll get it right soon, I promise."

"Soon? You need to get it right now or you're gone. I don't know why Kaede-san hired you, but you can be replaced in a second."

Yuna turned around, slamming her heels into the tile floor as she stormed off.

Mie sat at the circular table alone. The other girls in the hostess club were laughing, clinking glasses of expensive champagne, linking arms with the customers. And, most importantly, getting them to buy more drinks.

Makoto—or was his name Riku?—came back from the bathroom and landed in the seat next to Mie. She felt the booth's plastic cushioned seat shift under his weight.

"I missed you so much!" Mie said with a sprinkle of sugar in her voice that turned her stomach upside down and nearly made her vomit.

The man wheezed and patted some sweat off his forehead with a napkin. "Uh, oh yeah, sure."

Silence as thick as wading through mud.

"So, what do you do for work?" she asked, making sure to sit up straight and smile wide.

He yawned and looked at his watch.

"Um, how about another drink?" She asked.

The man shouted across the busy club, "Hey, can I get the check?"

"Did I do something wrong?" she asked in a hushed tone while looking over her shoulder at Yuna's cast-iron face, peering out at her from behind another customer's shoulders.

The man cocked his head to the side like his neck lost the ability to hold up his head. "What?"

Mie's eyes were filling up with tears that threatened to spill out over her face. On top of losing another customer, she couldn't bear the shame of having to run through the club with her cheap mascara running down to her chin.

"Please, sir, I need this job."

But it was too late. Makoto, Riku, whatever the hell his name was, was already heaving himself out of the booth and making his way over to the front podium to pay. It wouldn't be a large bill: he ordered a single drink for himself but none for Mie.

She knew she wasn't cut out for this. Wearing a dress that clung too tightly to her hips and revealed too much of her legs. Making conversation with men who refused to put forth any effort to talk back. Their eyes said enough as they raced up and down her figure. She longed to run back to her bedroom and hug her stuffed marshmallow pillow and scream her frustration into it. But what good would that do if there was no room to run back to? Technically there was, the apartment was still hers for the next few weeks based off her last rent payment. But it really wasn't hers anymore. She didn't believe in ghosts, but the memory of Sota's last action of life left a stain on that place. Glued inside the walls. Naked. Smiling. Even in her dreams, she kept seeing that eye. Yellow and black and wet.

I have to keep this job, it's the only way.

She just started working at the Golden Swan Club yesterday. Hostess gigs like this were easy enough to land, the money was good, and she needed tons to move out of her current place.

The hard clack of Yuna's heels assaulted her ears. She was coming up to Mie's table from behind, surely on her way to chew Mie out, possibly even convince Kaede-san to fire her.

Before Yuna could arrive, another woman jumped in front of her and sat by Mie. Hiromi Tanaka, by far the prettiest girl in the club, to Mie at least. Something about Hiromi comforted Mie, made her feel at home in this new harsh environment. Yuna turned on her stiletto heels and walked away.

"Another one got away, huh?"

"Oh, yeah. He wasn't happy with me, was he?"

Hiromi smiled. All teeth, white and dazzling. Smile lines creased over her face as she spoke, convincing Mie of her sincerity.

"Don't worry about it. And don't worry about her," she nodded over in Yuna's direction. "She hates all the new girls because she's jealous. And if Kaede-san likes you, that's all that matters."

"I still can't believe that. I mean, why did she hire me? I'm nothing special."

Hiromi stopped smiling. "Don't question her, okay? Trust her judgement. She knows what she's doing." Her smile sparked to life again. "And if she likes you, I like you. You'll get the hang of this in time. But don't be fake, I saw how you tried flattering that man earlier. They know they're paying for our attention, but they don't want to be reminded of it while they're here."

"Thank you."

Bells chimed and both women turned their heads as the front door opened. A man with slicked-back hair and what looked like a cashmere-silk suit walked in. He had a white feather sticking out of his chest pocket. From out of the backrooms, Kaede-san appeared, for the first time that night. She was wearing a silvery white kimono that glowed in the light. Her hair was tied up with four white roses pinning it in place. Her skin was fair and pale. She glided across the floor like her feet never touched it.

Kaede-san met the man at the entrance and bowed to him. He smiled and the dazzle of his teeth seemed to lighten up the room. Mie felt an immediate pull towards the man. Not attraction in any sexual way, there was something deeper and more visceral in the longing that sprang out of her heart just then. She actually blushed.

"Who is that?" she asked Hiromi.

Kaede-san led the man to the VIP table at the head of the room and sat him down. He leaned back in the booth and looked out over the club, nodding his head to whatever she was saying to him.

"He's Kageyama-san. Works for the White Feather Club."

Mie laughed. "And he puts an actual white feather in his suit?"

Hiromi put her finger to her lips. "Mie, he's an extremely valued guest. He doesn't come here to flirt and drink like everyone else. He scouts out girls to bring over to his club. He rotates around all the joints in Kiyamachi looking for the next star." Her eyes glistened with hope while her voice darkened with despair. "And he's never chosen me. Or anyone I know who's ever worked here."

"Is his place really that much better than here?"

Hiromi was staring off in the distance, nobody home. Mie repeated herself and Hiromi came back to reality. "Umm, what? Oh yeah. It's *the* place if you want to make it in this business. No low-life customers. I hear they only serve top politicians and famous people. A few girls who've worked there have gone on to do movies and stuff."

Mie couldn't believe what she was hearing. Just a week ago, she would have laughed if she knew she'd be working as a hostess. Even if just part-time. That alone was an alien enough concept. But movies? Dream jobs? She looked around the Golden Swan club and all she saw were sweaty men with flushed red faces and a darkened room, so no one would notice the stains on the curtains. And of course girls like Yuna—pretty on the outside but with the personality of a velociraptor just under the surface. How could anyone want to excel in this?

Hiromi grabbed her arm so quickly, Mie nearly screamed. "And I've heard he does VIP parties. If you get invited to one, you're set for life."

Kageyama caught Mie staring at him. Their eyes locked. Hiromi kept saying more meaningless words. All the conversations at nearby tables became muffled. Mie blocked everything out. She imagined herself getting invited to that party. Not only moving out of that apartment but getting a real house somewhere in the countryside. Quitting her daycare job. Growing sweet potatoes or corn or whatever else it was people did in idyllic rural settings.

For the first time in years, she imagined a future for herself.

Before she broke Kageyama's eye contact, one thing bothered her.

She thought she saw a flash of yellow in his eyes.

Mie walked into her apartment slightly drunk. She hadn't gotten many customers tonight, but even just a few drinks—even watered down ones—were enough to send her head spinning. She slipped off her heels and rubbed the sore skin by her ankles. It had been years since she'd worn shoes like these. Not since college, anyway.

She flipped on the lights. For a moment, she stood in the entryway, hesitating. Everything looked much the same as it always had. Flat screen TV, dresser, mounds of pink stuffed animals, and a shin-high coffee table in the one-room apartment. Not much more than that, really. She laughed at herself; at the fact that all her possessions, all she owned, could fit in this one space.

She wished she could just keep standing by the door and sleep there. Stepping any further into the room was like walking into a nuclear power plant in meltdown. Something had contaminated the space. More than just a memory of what was done, the radioactive fallout of the neighbor's bizarre actions seemed to soak into everything, pink bunnies included. There was no choice, though. She had no money, no family, and no friends. Where else could she go but here?

Just tough it out for a little longer.

She walked forward and sat down on the floor by her foldout futon and got it ready for bed. Her usual ritual of the nightly bath hadn't happened for a week now. Not since *he* was discovered in the walls. Public bath houses saved her there. But she felt something was missing from her life. A comforting nightly routine that was now contaminated. Ruined by the actions of one man. She vowed to never enter that bathroom again. Even if she had to pee at three am, she'd just walk down the street and do it at a convenience store.

She undressed, cleaned off her makeup with a cleansing wipe, turned off the lights, and went to bed.

Her mind drifted up to the ceiling and beyond. It floated out to the Golden Swan Club. Hiromi's smile and Yuna's scowl. How long could she last there? Not long without Hiromi, that was for sure. Her mind moved beyond that tiny club and into the stratosphere. She imagined

what the White Feather Club looked like. She saw clouds holding up a
silver mansion, like some sort of heaven.

In it was more than riches, it was a life that held meaning.

She dreamt about the house she would build by a rice paddy, the
cocker spaniel she'd get to keep her company, the peace and quiet that
money could buy. She was sitting in a rocking chair on a large porch,
looking out at the pink and purple sunset gracing low hills as if melting
off the sky. Happiness filled the moment. Until the black shape started
rising from the waters of the rice field in front of her. Yellow eyes. Forked
tongue. Something large slithered out of the water and made its way
towards her.

Nine of them.

Then came the scratching.

It broke her out of her dream so harshly that she sat up straight in
the futon, cold sweat wrapping around her thin arms. It was a slight
scuttling sound. Not a dream. Like mice running. Inside the wall near
the bathroom.

It stopped.

Am I hearing things?

Fear shook her whole body. She reached for her phone and turned on
the flashlight. In the bright spotlight, she saw her animals, her TV, her
coffee table, the walls, the bathroom door, the kitchen sink.

No more sounds. Nothing out of the ordinary. Just the radioactive
stain of Sota Kobayashi, permeating her once-safe place. She might even
burn her old clothes and even the body pillow in the corner. Start over
new.

Body pillow?

Mie's blood froze solid in her veins. She didn't own a body pillow. The
long dark shape seemed to writhe and undulate in the shadows. Like the

thing in her dreams. She flashed the light over by the corner once more. Nothing there but her stuffed rabbit.

Her phone rang.

"Shit!"

She clutched her chest, and her heartbeat shot through the roof. The adrenaline was enough to put some movement back in her legs, and the first thing she did was spring to her feet and slam on the lights. Then she answered the call.

It was Kaede-san.

At five in the morning.

Told her to not come in to work tonight.

Instead, she was expected at the White Feather Club for their VIP party.

Hope dispelled her fears. She couldn't get back to sleep.

Mie stepped out of the limousine and into the frigid air. The icy wind bit at her exposed thighs and cut through the little protection her parka provided her. Light snow fell over the streets. It melted almost immediately after hitting the asphalt, but it was nice to see brief moments of change come over the city. The golden lights of the nearby restaurants looked like little flames providing shelter on the cold winter night. She stood before a five-story building with no windows, save for one on the top floor. The front of the building was well lit, showing off a marble white architecture to the narrow street, crowded as it was with other establishments.

Mie noticed the people who walked into these places. Every last one of them dressed like royalty. Mink fur scarves. Suede suits. Limos and personal drivers. This was a neighborhood she could never have imagined having access to. This was a world apart from her upbringing in rural Niigata, where the largest building in town was the old city hall.

She ascended the white stone steps that led up to the golden front doors. Five other women were waiting out front, each of them shivering with their hands in their parka and jacket pockets. Four of the women were beyond beautiful. Their collective breath hung over their heads like a cloud. Dressed in scarlet, gold, purple, and black dresses under their coats. Intimidation immediately overwhelmed Mie. The woman in red gave her a half-second glance and scoffed. The fifth woman looked plainer to Mie, more on her level, more down to earth.

She was dressed in a white dress, and something about the way she carried herself put Mie at ease. Maybe it was the slight smile that made its home on her lips. As Mie drew near, she questioned why she was chosen out of all the girls in the club. Yuna and Hiromi weren't here, and she hadn't heard from them all day. As far as she knew, none of the girls at the Golden Swan were going to be here tonight.

Mie climbed the last step and stood beside the woman in white. Their eyes met and they both bowed their heads, but nobody spoke as they waited for the door to open. Mie sensed the nervous energy bouncing between them in the cold. The club looked like a palace. She never would have imagined such a place could exist in the cramped alleyways of Kyoto. It almost didn't make sense how big the building looked. She knew that there was a river on the other side of the club, and the neighboring businesses didn't look like they occupied much land at all.

The doors opened.

A short man in a black suit, white gloves, and an earpiece welcomed them.

"Ladies, thank you for waiting. Please follow me to the fifth floor where the party will begin. Do not touch anything you see, do not wander off, do not talk. Once we arrive, the schedule for the night will be explained to you."

Mie wanted to make eye contact with the woman in white, to check for some mutual understanding. Maybe she would say, "Yeah, this is weird, let's get out of here." But the woman kept her eyes forward and Mie was left to her own thoughts as they walked into the club and the doors shut behind them.

She was grateful to be wrapped in the warmth of the interior. It felt like a fire was burning, she could even hear the crackle of the flames but couldn't see where the sound or the heat was coming from.

Probably just speakers and a radiator.

The walls were spotless white – marble, she thought. The skirting boards were painted gold. Every once in a while, they walked past a white statue. One was of a woman in a cloak, holding a baby in her arms. Another was of two lovers, holding hands and gazing into each other's eyes.

An elevator door – gold, of course – opened, and they all entered. All of them remained silent as the elevator went up. Mie didn't dare try to make eye contact with anyone. The air in that space felt somehow thicker, like they were underwater. She felt pressure build in her head until her ears popped like they did when Mom took her on trips along high mountain roads.

The elevator stopped at the fifth floor. Doors opened. The man led them out into a lounge area with a high domed ceiling. So high, it seemed like the building should have been seven stories tall from the outside, not five. Golden partitions taller than they were crisscrossed the large room, making it impossible to see the whole space. A sweet lavender smell beckoned them to enter. Music played from speakers set high in the walls. Strings like a harp or a Shamisen.

They walked around a partition and came to an open space with three large purple cushioned sofas.

"Please, take a seat and Kageyama-san will be with you shortly. And do remember, refrain from speaking with one another."

The man turned around and disappeared behind a partition with a red swan pattern emblazoned on its side.

Mie sat with her back straight like she was taught back in school. Nice and proper-like. All the girls in class had to sit like this while the boys got to hunch over like trolls and not get yelled at by the teacher.

The woman in white sat next to her on the sofa.

The other women–sitting over at a different sofa–darted their eyes in her direction for the briefest of moments, but she still felt the judgment in those glances.

She noticed another statue off to her left against the wall. It was black marble and was of a nine-headed snake, its tail coiled around a woman, her mouth open in a frozen scream.

Mie felt sick looking at it.

A few minutes later, Kageyama-san appeared. His black hair slicked back. Wearing a tuxedo. His square jaw and blazingly white teeth, his smile, all made him exceedingly attractive. But his eyes were somewhat sunken. Bright in the dark hollows of his face. Mie was half-relieved this meant an end to the silence, and of having to look at that statue, but also half-afraid that now this meant the night was getting started. Flirting with men for money was one thing. She hoped nothing else was expected.

"Ladies, thank you for coming. And thank you for saying yes to our invitation to work here." He flashed that chalk-white smile at them. That warm feeling stirred in Mie's stomach, the same as it did last night.

"What are the clients like?" asked the woman in the red dress in an impatient tone. "And what's the pay like?"

Kageyama-san's bright eyes darkened. He stared deeply into the woman's eyes. She went on, "You can't expect us to work without—"

He snapped his fingers. Two men came out from behind the partition and approached the red-dress woman. They stood on either side of her and gripped her arms.

"What the fuck?" she yelled at them and tried to use her purse to bat them away.

"Let this be a lesson to the rest of you," Kageyama-san said. "Follow instructions."

The men lifted the woman in the red dress off the sofa, one man holding each of her arms.

They carried her away as she kicked and yelled profanities at them. Kageyama-san winced at the sound of her voice until it grew smaller and then altogether silent as the elevator doors closed.

Mie's heart raced. She could feel a cold sweat forming on her brow.

Kageyama-san cleared his throat. "I apologize for that barbarous act. But I must impose on you the seriousness of this job. Our clients are not like any men you have met before. They are not CEOs, politicians, or movie actors. Theirs is a higher, older, and more important profession. And they prefer things to be done the old way. That means – and this should be easy for you – no talking. At all. They will talk to you and all you have to do is listen to them and pour their drinks. Don't even laugh when they laugh. No sounds at all. Easy, yes? If you perform well tonight, one of you may even be chosen as the White Feather, the greatest honor that can be bestowed on a woman. You will also have to change into some kimonos we have on hand."

Five young women dressed in dazzling white and red dress rushed in, each holding out a kimono in their hands. In movements far too quick for Mie to register, someone moved the partition nearest her so that it bent forward, cutting her off from the other two sofas. She sat alone with the woman in the white dress as two of the younger girls held out the new clothes for them to change into. Mie took the clothes tentatively and smiled at the woman in white. She smiled back. Both of them were clearly embarrassed. Mie undressed and put the kimono on. The servant girl helped her tie off the sash at her waist.

When she was finished, Mie turned around and saw the woman in the white dress now wearing a white kimono. Mie wanted to ask her name but remembered the rule. She looked down and saw that her new clothing matched the color of her turquoise skirt she had on earlier. The partitions opened and revealed the other three women, all wearing kimono the same color as their previous dresses. Purple, gold, and black. The sofas were pulled away and three servant girls pulled out a large *tatami* mat the size of a swimming pool from another room and laid it across the floor. In moments, they set down pillows and low-lying tables.

"Okay, ladies, please sit on your knees near one of the tables. The guests have just arrived downstairs and will be up here in a moment." He made as if to turn away but stopped. "None of you can play a shamisen, can you?"

The woman in the white kimono raised her hand and almost spoke but caught herself in time

"Ah, Tachibana-san. Good to know. One of our guests loves music, so we will pair him with you."

One of the servant girls pulled the instrument from behind a partition and rushed it over. She kneeled in front of Tachibana-san, and the latter nervously grabbed the shamisen.

Mie went to her knees and sat at the table nearest her. She hadn't sat on her knees in *seiza* style in years and worried how long she could stay on her knees while entertaining these "guests". She wondered who they could be. The entire situation was odd, the oddest thing to happen to her after the man in her bathroom wall.

The elevator doors opened. The servant girls pulled the partitions back and Mie could see the doors clearly.

Nine men came into the room, led by the doorman from earlier. The guests looked almost indistinguishable from each other. Each of them was clad in a deep purple kimono with blue belts around their pot bellies. They wore wooden sandals that clicked like hooves on the hardwood floor. They were clean-shaven and completely bald. They looked like men who had just come off a movie set about samurai. She had to hold her breath to keep from laughing.

The men took their seats by the women on the tatami. Two sat down cross-legged in front of Mie. She bowed her head low and almost said "hello." Her silence wasn't because she suddenly remembered the rule just then, it was that she saw what the men had attached to their belts.

Swords. In their scabbards and clipped onto their sash belts.

The men took their swords out and laid them on the ground and bowed back to her.

Neither of the men spoke. They stared at Mie, but not in the way other men had back at the Golden Swan, scanning her body. No, these men stared right into her eyes, not blinking once.

She wanted to look away but smiled politely instead. A servant girl placed some hot tea and two cups on the table. Mie grabbed the kettle and poured the tea into both cups. She lifted one with both hands and offered it to the man nearest her, the one with eyebrows that had grown wildly out of control. He took the cup and said, "thank you." She gave the other cup to the other man, the one with a round face and kind eyes. He said nothing but smiled at her. She smiled back.

Maybe this isn't so bad. At least I don't have to talk.

Mie heard the men at the next table talking to the girl in the purple kimono. They were asking her her age. Mie tensed and waited to hear if she would respond. She didn't. But the men didn't seem angry. They chuckled and began speaking to each other instead.

The two men in front of Mie said nothing. They sipped their tea and stared at her. The round-faced man fiddled with his sword with a twitching hand. She did her best to keep that smile fixed to her face. She alternated between keeping their eye contact and looking away when it became too intense. Warm golden light filled the room from the lights overhead. It might have been just that; their eyes might have been tinged with the light. But the more Mie saw of their eyes, the more yellow they became. She looked down at her tea, at the swirling bits of leaves in the cup. The specks reminded her of the black in Sota's eye. Floating around.

No, it wasn't the light, she decided. Something was off with these men, and it wasn't just awkwardness. They were staring at her, so why not stare back? She held their eyes with her own. There was no white in their eyes. All yellow. Like a snake's. They didn't blink. Their pupils seemed to narrow and take an almost diamond shape.

A trick of the low light?

The man with the long eyebrows finally spoke. "What do you think?"

The round-faced man replied, "Maybe. That other one playing the music might be better. I like her innocence."

Mie hadn't even noticed that Tachibana-san had started playing the shamisen somewhere behind her.

The eyebrow man said, "We'll see."

They never took their eyes off Mie, even as they spoke about Tachibana-san. Their eyes seemed to widen. Red veins grew brighter in the wet yellow of their eyeballs. She even saw the round-faced man flick his tongue in and out for a moment.

"Gentlemen," Kageyama-san said as he stood in the middle of the room. "The time has come for the arrow."

The men laughed and applauded and slapped each other on the shoulders. One of the servant girls ran out and took a knee in front of Kageyama-san. She was holding a bow and a single, white-feathered arrow in her hands.

The nine guests stood and walked over to the side of the room, leaving their swords on the ground. For a moment, she thought about walking out then and there, screw the money. This was too weird. But she didn't.

Kageyama-san took the bow in his hands and strung the arrow. Another servant girl blindfolded him with a red sash and then spun him around twice.

He pointed the arrow at Mie's face. She felt her heart fall into her stomach like a glacier melting into the sea. He moved to his left and pointed it at the woman in the black kimono. She gasped. One by one, Kageyama-san aimed the arrow at each of the women.

The nine guests leered and smiled. One man even had both hands on his knees, leaning forward, watching with anticipation.

Kageyama-san pointed the arrow at the ceiling and let it fly loose. The arrow shot straight up and then arched forward, towards the women. The tail end of the arrow quivered, and it almost seemed to float instead of fall down. It landed right in front of Tachibana-san. The arrowhead stuck in the tatami mat right at her feet. She almost dropped the shamisen.

The men erupted in an avalanche of applause and cheers. Mie felt that pressure build inside her head again. If Tachibana-san was afraid, she didn't show it, she kept that smile on her face. Mie's face was twisted in horror and disgust: there would be no more hiding how she felt about this place.

They shot an arrow that could have killed someone.

For fun?

Kageyama-san removed his blindfold and smiled. "Tachibana-san, congratulations, you have been chosen to stay on as a permanent employee of the White Feather Club. Please, step forward."

She put down the instrument, rose, walked to the middle of the room, and bowed to the guests.

"The rest of you ladies, thank you for your time, but your services are no longer required. You will each be wired five hundred thousand yen to your accounts in the morning. Please change and then gather your belongings and vacate the premises. And remember, no talking on your way out. You will all be required to sign a legally binding waiver at the front door to never discuss tonight's events. If you do so, we will take action. Goodbye."

With that, the partitions came flying back into the center of the room and divided each of the women alone with a servant girl. They picked up the swords and handed them back to the men.

The girl in front of Mie handed her back her clothes. Mie got dressed as the girl turned around. The girl handed her her purse and made a gesture for her to leave. The partition opened and she saw a clear hall leading back to the elevator.

As she walked back to the exit, a flood filled her mind. The money was beyond amazing, enough to move out tomorrow and get a new place anywhere in the city that she wanted. She could quit the Golden Swan.

But the arrow? The men with swords? The rule against speaking?

What did that have to do with her anymore?

As she was within an arm's reach of the elevator, the rest of the women, minus Tachibana-san, slipped through a gap in the partitions and joined her. In that gap, Mie saw the men surrounding Tachibana-san; her once-serene face now stretched out in horror. One of the men had taken off his robe, revealing a back tattoo of a nine-headed serpent. The partition closed.

This isn't right.

Her head swam with conflicting thoughts.

Leave now and be done with this place.

But her face? She looked so scared.

You don't even know her. And what can you even do?

The elevator doors opened and the short man in the suit appeared from inside the elevator. The other women filed in. Mie heard a whimper—quickly muffled— from behind the partitions. She went in the elevator anyway. The doors closed. The elevator descended to the first floor. Her heart pounded against her ribs, threatening to crack them. She knew what she was going to do, and the thought of that action terrified her. She counted on being overlooked. The doors opened and the man exited the elevator. The women followed. He didn't even turn around to make sure they had all gotten off. Mie stayed behind and hit the button for the fifth floor.

The woman in the purple dress turned and looked at her just before the doors closed.

She said nothing.

The elevator went up. Each floor she passed felt like an eternity. She almost wished the doors would never open. That way, she could exist in this limbo of indecision forever. She thought about aborting her plan and heading back down.

But the whimper.

Tachibana-san's face.

Mie didn't want to imagine what was happening upstairs and had no idea what she could even do about it. But under all that fear, there was a rage. She remembered the eye in the wall. The man who spied on her for who knows how long. She let go of her apartment and counted it as lost because of the stain of *his* hideous actions.

But this has nothing to do with me.

The doors opened. The partitions blocked any view of the center of the room.

Mie heard another muffled cry. The sound of something heavy being dragged across the floor. *Was that a water sprinkler?*

The sound of a slap.

It could just be sex. Why are you still waiting here? Nothing to do with you.

Then Tachibana-san cried out, "No!"

A growl.

Tables turned and tossed aside.

The sound of her weeping.

Mie gripped the edge of a partition and opened it. Whatever was happening was blocked off by another wall. But in front of her on the floor were the robes of the nine guests. And their swords. With shaking hands, she picked up one of the swords and unsheathed it. She neared the last partition.

Mie heard a hiss.

She grabbed the partition and slowly pushed it open.

This was not what she was expecting.

Before her was a large black mass. It was undulating and coiling around the center of the room. It *filled* the room. She couldn't process what this was. Until she saw Tachibana-san in the dead center of the room, eyes opened and staring at the ceiling, her body sliding into the unhinged jaw of a giant snake. The other eight heads rose from the ground and set their yellow eyes on Mie.

She ran back to the elevator, holding the sword out in front of her. The doors opened and the doorman ran out, right into the blade as it buried itself deep in his stomach. Mie screamed and let go of the handle. In response to her cry, the creature behind her hissed and recoiled from her. The doorman slid back against the wall, smearing it red.

Mie ran into the elevator and feverishly slammed the ground floor button. A large black and scaled head pushed the partitions to the ground. It raced towards the elevator.

"No!" Mie screamed at it. The thing stopped moving, shut its eyes, and jerked its head to the side. Almost like it ran into an invisible wall. "Stay away!"

With those words, the thing recoiled again and hissed. Flicked out its purple tongue and widened its yellow eyes in hate. The doors shut and the elevator went down to the ground floor.

They opened it and she ran out into the street. She kept running until she reached the nearest police station.

The whole time those yellow eyes flashed in her mind.

Even when she closed her eyes. There they were.

In the time it took to run to the nearest police station she came to realize: those eyes would never leave her.

TORNAQ

J ean rowed the canoe across the still waters of the lake. The air lashed his cheeks and the skin around his eyes with the threat of frostbite. He set out from his camp only a few hours ago, around eleven in the afternoon. Way out here the midday stars looked so close and so clear that he could reach up and pluck them out of the sky. The pale blue twilight lasted long enough for him to find his way to the village, but now the sun was gone. A silent and frozen night swallowed the day.

True peace.

The smoke from his tobacco pipe washed over his eyes, stinging them yet providing him moments of relief from the cold. At least there were no mosquitoes this time of year.

He loved it though. This life. The only sound the paddle slicing through the still water. No wife telling him to lay off the drink. No task master expecting him to show up at the docks at a certain time on a certain day. Just him, the occasional animal, and the wide-open nothingness of the tundra.

A man could lose himself out here, or so he was told when he picked up work as a fur trapper two years ago. Lose himself and never be found again. And that was precisely what he meant to do.

Only on rare occasions did he need to return to civilization to restock. He could fish well enough and had plenty to eat even in the depths of winter. His boots though, they needed a mend he wasn't able to perform himself. Got them caught on jagged rocks last week as he was chasing after some caribou. The stone ripped right through them. His ankle too, but that didn't matter much to him. A skin-deep cut that hurt like hell but didn't hinder him walking.

The sudden shadow of land seemed to come out of nowhere, like an assaulting whale threatening to breach itself over his vessel. Normally, several bonfires would be sending out embers to light up the shore in pulsing orange waves. The village now was encased in darkness. The faint tease of a tree line was further back.

Jean tapped his pipe against the side of the canoe and set it down by his pack. He stopped paddling and strained his ears. The wind groaned and howled. But he could hear no people. No dogs. He saw no shadows walking by the shore. Only the black vague shapes of the homes dotting the land. This was the right spot, he was sure of it.

Jean instinctively picked up his rifle and made sure it was loaded. He resumed paddling, quietly, until his canoe touched the rocky shore. He got out and stood still. No sound save for the wind. It caused the trees in the distance to creak and crack. Almost like something was walking in the forest.

Jean pulled the canoe fully onto the beach. He felt the blood course through his muscles again, giving him the illusion of warmth.

He almost called out for Sukak, the only man in this world he considered a friend. Almost one anyway. Jean passed through this village several times a year when he needed something. He would never admit company was one of those things. Sukak was a barrel-chested man with a weather worn face, much like himself. Neither man said much, but Jean had to admit he enjoyed smoking next to him, silently, warming themselves by a fire, and roasting fish.

He didn't call out though. The cold was a common enough thing that he altogether ignored it. Yet, somehow, he felt his blood run even colder just then. The hairs on his arm stood up like needles under his woolen coat. He shouldered his rifle and listened. Nothing but the damn wind screeching off in the distance.

He grabbed an oil lamp from the canoe and lit it. The light brought to life everything immediately in front of him in a quivering yellow halo. Beyond that, a desolate void. Anything could run up to him and he would see nothing until it was already within that circle of light.

He thought about leaving. Damn the boot to hell, he'd figure something out, he always did. It might have been friendship, it might have been love, maybe even just respect, whatever it was, Jean felt compelled to look for Sukak and his family.

Something was not right.

Jean left the beach, light in one hand, gun in the other, and passed the first *tupiq* to his right. He leaned in to listen but heard nothing inside. In front of the entrance to the tent a pot was strung up over ashes and blackened wood. He bent down and touched the side of the pot.

Cold.

The soup inside was solid ice.

He lifted the tent flap. The lamp cast its golden light around the home. No people. He went in and looked around. He found a fur lined jacket for a child and a hunting knife; items a family would never leave behind.

He left the tent and moved further into the village. Most of the homes were *igloo* and fresh snow covered the ground. The Moon reflected off the snow, helping him see the outline of the environment. In the near stillness, the village gave off a ghostly glow. He found that he could see distance better without the lamp's light so he moved it to his side.

Beyond the homes, was the black outline of the forest. Like smudges of soot spread over a burnt canvas. The spaces in between the trees were too dark to see anything.

Jean gripped the rifle to the point where he thought he could snap it in half even with just the one hand. As he moved, the crunch of the crystallized snow made him wince. He was giving away his position. Giving it away to what?

He looked down and made out tracks. Boot prints both large and small. Nothing odd, just the footprints of the people who lived here. He was on the lookout for polar bear tracks in particular. There was no blood on the snow. No bodies. None of the homes looked broken into. Besides, a single bear was no match for an entire village. They had dogs and guns here.

Jean came upon Sukak's igloo. In front of the entrance, another pot of food, the metal cold to the touch. A ladle rested inside. Several bowls were on the snow below it. Some frozen meat spilled over the ground.

Jean entered the igloo. The first thing he noticed, to his right, leaning up against the wall, was a rifle. He set the lamp and his own gun down and inspected his friend's firearm. Loaded. Not a single shot fired from it. He put it back against the wall and picked up his things.

"Wer are ya? Ya ol' bastad. Wer'd y'all go?"

Too afraid to let his voice rise above a whisper, he had to let it out. If he didn't find a release valve for the growing dread in his stomach, he felt it might devour him from the inside out.

His mind ran through the possibilities. It couldn't have been as simple as moving camp. All of their things, the food, the guns, the snowshoes, all necessary for survival were still laying around. No bodies, no sign of attack; could they have all left, empty-handed, into the tundra? That would be suicide.

Jean left the *igloo*.

Only one last place to check. He knew if anyone was away from the camp they'd never last long in the sub-zero temperatures. It would be useless to go out looking *out there*. At least he wouldn't do it alone. *Go back into Fort Smith and get some help tomorrow*.

Jean made his way over to the dogs. Whenever he had visited in the past, he would hear their yapping and howling and excited whining. Quiet now. A slightly sweet mixed with raw sewage and rotten eggs smell struck him. It made him gag as waves of nausea overtook him. Jean pressed on and rounded the last igloo of the village. The twelve sled dogs, unchained, lay in frozen heaps on the ground. Jean ran over the crackling snow to the closest one and set his lamp and rifle down. He felt around the animal's chest for any sign of life.

There was none. The body was nearly frozen solid. Its ribs were like steel and its stomach shrunken. No wounds, no blood. He checked on a few of the others. All the same. These dogs had starved to death. How?

There was food right there, in front of every home. And these dogs were not restrained.

Jean's heart beat faster. He felt a heaviness in the crisp air. Almost like a blizzard had descended on the village. But it wasn't snowing. The wind picked up and blew some snow off the ground and whipped it around his face. The cold stung his skin like thousands of needles. He grabbed his things, got up, and started back to the canoe. A quick movement to his left jolted him to a stop. He turned towards it, rifle aimed and ready. The lamp's light couldn't reach what he was trying to make out in the distance. But it was something large; he heard the heavy footfall in the snow, he saw the towering shadow move further back.

He fired the rifle.

The deafening blast felt obscene in the quiet, almost sacred, landscape. He shot another round. Then he waited. Listened.

The wind died down as if to assist him. There were no footsteps, if the first had even happened. He moved forward to see if he hit anything.

The light revealed more than a dozen piles of stone and two Christian crosses made of wood. He knew from previous visits that this was the cemetery, built close to camp so that the dead were never forgotten. One of the rock piles had been scattered across the snow. He drew near and saw that a hole had been dug up where the body once lay. He shined the light into the grave.

Nothing there.

The other burial mounds were intact, just this one had been vandalized, or was it some ritual or ceremony he couldn't hope to understand? Surely the dead don't release themselves?

Jean recalled the last time he was here. Sukak told him that six people had died of a disease, far more than usual. He even saw them pray over the graves out here. He felt sick in his stomach at the thought that there could be a connection.

Jean looked out in the dark tundra, the infinite flat expanse beyond the village, one last time. The wind screeched like a woman. It then morphed into the cries of a child. He knew that these lonely nights could warp a man's mind and it was best to not listen. Your mind could make you hear anything out here. He shut his eyes and shook his head.

Whatever happened here was over. There was nobody left. He feared for his friend but what more could be done?

It was time to leave.

Jean picked up his pace and re-entered the village. He missed it the first time, his back to the igloos as he walked out to the dogs. Coming back, he could clearly see it now. Claw marks scratched into the ice of an igloo. He put the lamp's handle in his mouth and put his free hand up to the deep incisions. Each one was wide. Five in total. The slash marks were half the size of his palm.

This wasn't possible. No bear was that big. And where were the tracks?

Behind him, the crunching of snow. Not the light sounds his own feet were making. This was from something larger than a man. Something so close he dared not turn to face it. The heavy air intensified. He began sweating. His chest felt like it was caving in on itself. His lungs filled up with an icy cold that burned.

Jean put the lamp back in his hand and walked, half-jogged, towards the beach, careful not to run and give the predator cause to chase.

Another footstep weighed down into the snow. Then another. Whatever it was, it was moving slowly. Gently, even. Jean walked faster and came to the tents near the shore. He reloaded his rifle as he moved, nearly dropping the lamp. He could see the dark outline of his canoe on the beach. The footsteps rushed forward with intensity. Barreling towards him. Jean yelled and dropped the lamp. He spun around and aimed his gun.

At nothing.

His ankle, up until now deciding not to bother him, kicked up a mighty complaint. The skin felt like it had ripped open.

"Fuck." He let out and held onto his ankle.

The footsteps came in rushing to his left.

He let loose another shot from the rifle.

Jean felt for his lamp at his feet, but the light had gone out. His only shield against the unseen -- gone. Jean was left in the ethereal glow of the snow.

He backed up, shuffling towards his boat, not taking his eyes off the darkness, else something should move and take chase once more.

A thick black cloud, like ink spreading up a paper, took form in front of him. It could have been his eyes playing tricks on him, but he could have sworn he saw it moving, prowling, just beyond his ability to see.

A deep growl ripped through the darkness. It came from all directions. The vibration of its tone nearly caused him to vomit. He felt it in his bones.

This was no bear.

Jean fired two more rounds into the dark.

A splash in the water.

He turned in time to see his canoe being lifted up to the sky. In a moment it was gone. Disappeared into the black night. He heard another splash from further way, out towards the middle of the lake. The water started bubbling up as if boiling.

Jean dropped the rifle and fell shaking to his knees.

A word came to his mouth from an unknown compulsion. Like a bottled fire kept locked away in his gut. It clawed up his throat and forced itself out of his mouth. He didn't know what it meant or why he was saying it. The words burned his mouth as he spoke.

"Tornaq."

He looked up to the sky and felt a sudden rush of air burst over his face. Like he was falling off a cliff.

His body felt weightless, and he was spun around as if caught in a riptide. When he stopped moving, he was staring down at the village. His vision was blurred, and he was dizzy. When he could focus his sight, he let out a cry. He could see the village clearly now.

From high up.

The land was getting smaller.

THE FACE

"**W**ake up!"

Lucy bolted out of bed like she had been electrocuted. Jacob flipped the lights on and slammed the bedroom door shut.

Adrenaline—much better than coffee—brought her to her senses quickly. "What's going on?"

"The police. We need to call them now!"

He took hold of a nearby dresser, dragged it to the door, and barricaded it.

He flashed Lucy a wild expression, one she had never seen before in her son's eyes. It reminded her of the time she nearly hit a deer while driving too fast at night.

"Mom! Now! Call them!"

She jumped out of the bed and fumbled for her phone on the nightstand. As she started dialing 110, Jacob flipped the mattress up and against the window by the headboard of the bed. The mattress struck the lights on the ceiling and almost sent them crashing down. He slipped and struggled as he pushed until he eventually got it up and leaning against the glass.

On the phone a woman answered in Japanese. Fuck. Of course she would, but Lucy, in her heightened panic, briefly thought she was back in California.

"Uh, *tasukete,* help, *kudasai!*" Lucy was able to get out.

The woman on the line spoke, presumably asking for more details, Lucy could give none. She covered the phone's receiver and looked at Jacob, "What is happening? Tell me."

Jacob was bouncing back and forth, looking at the room's two windows, unable to calm down. "There was a face at the window downstairs. Just-just, tell them to hurry!"

Lucy knew just enough Japanese to convey her address to the woman on the line and then she hung up.

Lucy ran over to her son and put her hands on his shoulders. He was already a good foot taller than she was, but that look on his face made him seem five years old again. All she wanted to do then was scoop him up in her arms.

"Where is your father?" Even as she spoke those words, her own heart sank into the ground. Why were they bordering up the room when Steve was still out there!? And what was happening?

Jacob was near convulsing. She could actually hear his teeth chattering.

"He-he went outside. I told him not to, but he tried to scare it away."

It?

Lucy let got of her son and went over to the door.

"Mom, no! We can't go out there!"

She could barely hear what he was saying. The rush of blood in her veins was too loud in her head. She took her hand off the dresser and turned to face Jacob.

"Tell me exactly what is going on."

Jacob glanced at the windows. One he had covered with the mattress. The other remained as it was, there was nothing to put over it. But they were on the second floor, why was he so worried?

"Dad was in his office working or something. I came downstairs to get some water and I noticed the lights for the deck were still on. And, I don't know, I just wanted to look outside. I opened the curtains and there was this, this face, right next to the glass! Like not even a foot away from me. I yelled and Dad ran over. He saw it too. He ran outside to chase it away, but he never came back."

Jacob started crying. As if speaking the words out loud sealed the finality of what had happened. Lucy's skin threatened to slide off her bones, she shivered so much.

"But Dad didn't see what I did. It wasn't a person! It was, like, this, I don't know, like someone was wearing a mask. I know it wasn't a mask. It had these fangs and these big red eyes and they blinked, it wasn't a mask, Mom! The face was huge! And Dad went out there and didn't come back!"

He sobbed and clung to Lucy's nightgown as she held onto him. She felt a rush of tears about to let loose but held them back by gritting her teeth. At fifteen years old her boy had instantly reverted back to being her baby. The one she had to protect at all costs. By any means necessary.

The police were on their way, she hoped. She also knew they wouldn't be here for another hour. And downstairs had two big glass doors.

Steve had brought them out to Japan just three months ago. He was obsessed with making a homestead and living off the land. Get away from the claustrophobic grind of Los Angeles and live out in nature. Ever since he quit his job at the firm, he was insistent on starting over again fresh. At first, so was she. It sounded fun. A perfect way to inject a little adventure back into their lives.

But she never liked it out here. From day one she had this feeling that things were just off in the woods. Their home was bought for next to nothing. The original owners had been dead for decades and the prefecture just wanted to unload the responsibility and the tax burden on somebody else. The home was hidden away in the mountains, surrounded by deep forests and hills that jutted straight out of the ground. With valleys of farmland between the peaks, nothing like she'd ever seen back in America.

The house itself was a shithole. Full of junk: rusted bicycles, moldy clothes, even candy wrappers. They spent the first week cleaning the thing and the next month renovating it. There was a fence around the property with tiny skulls nailed to it, things like squirrels or foxes maybe. They had a hell of a time ripping each one out. Honestly, they gave her the creeps.

Their closest neighbor was an old man named Makoto, he was a good five-minute drive, maybe a twenty-minute walk, up the road. Makoto had paid his respects when they moved in and gave them each a gift; a bag of hard candy for Jacob, a bottle of *sake* for Steve, and a bouquet of purple flowers for her. He spoke zero English but was kind enough.

He did take Steve aside that day and whispered something in his ears. Steve's Japanese was better than hers and he told her later that Makoto said to stay out of the woods. That they were dangerous. That things could follow them back. Steve laughed it off and even got angry when talking about it, thinking the locals were trying to scare them off.

Makoto told him to leave the skulls up or a bad thing would come.

A thought that the old man could be out there right now, in mask, terrorizing her family, made her sick with anger.

But no. Lucy, deep down, believed in Makoto. One day while she was planting potatoes in the backyard, covered in sweat and gritty soil, she had the sudden sensation of being watched. Like a cold wind kissed the back of her neck. She stood up and turned to look out at the trees. All of them grew closely together and wild grass filled in the gaps. There was no easy way to see inside. She could have sworn she saw a man in the darkest part of the forest, staring at her. She even saw a faint flash of red—*Big red eyes?*

Steve didn't believe her though. Said that she just wasn't used to living so far out in the mountains, and in a foreign country at that. "Try to relax and I promise you'll get used to it," he said.

Even Jacob didn't like this place. Not since last week when he went out alone on a trail and came across that creepy shrine. He told her he saw a deer skull nailed to a tree by this old and rotted wooden shrine. A fat and twisted tree hung over the shrine and he must have touched it, though he said he didn't remember, because his hands were covered in black sap when he returned.

Since that day, Jacob refused to go out alone. Said he felt like something was watching him from the forest, even as he slept. Hence why he moved his bedroom upstairs a few days ago.

Things ramped up to the point where Lucy thought about taking her son back to America if Steve wouldn't listen.

There was a fucking cow skull tied to a tree by our house! It wasn't there when we moved in!

And again, Steve played it off as not a problem.

"Okay, we need to think honey, the police are on their way, but it's going to take a while. You only saw one man? Did you see anyone else, or did he have a weapon?"

"It wasn't a man, Mom. It was a monster! The face, it was too big."

Jacob fell to his knees, and she tried to catch him.

Monster?

Lucy had to decide their course of action, right now. Stay in the room and hope the intruder wouldn't break in from downstairs, which they could easily do. Or make a run for their Jeep and book it to Makoto's.

No, that's too risky, stay put.

But what about Steve?

Monster?

Just then she heard Steve's voice from right outside the barricaded window.

"Lucy, are you there?"

Relief flooded her heart and the tension in her muscles relaxed. The sensation was euphoric compared to the stress of the last few minutes. Even Jacob stopped crying and rose to his feet, wiping the tears from his face. He smiled.

Lucy was about to move the mattress and address her husband until she realized: *why the hell is he talking to me from out there?*

"Honey!" She shouted through the mattress. "What are you doing out there?"

A rustle of grass from the backyard.

A grunt like a pig.

Heavy breathing.

"Lucy, are you there? Jacob, my boy, how you doing?"

Jacob's smile inverted.

Lucy's body tensed and she dug her fingertips into her palms. This was not the way Steve talked.

"Steve! Why don't you just come inside and talk to us?"

A light squeal and a stamping of feet from the yard.

"Lucy, are you there? Jacob, my boy, how you—" Grunting and a low moan. "How you, doing?" The last words came out in a voice Lucy had never heard in her life. It was deep like Steve's, but there was this underlying echo to it, like he was speaking in a large auditorium.

"Hello, hello, hello." Came the voice, matching Steve's perfectly once again. "Can I? I, come in. Can I come in?"

Jacob grabbed her nightgown's sleeve, just like he used to do when nightmares woke him up as a kid.

"Mom, that's not Dad, is it?"

"No, I don't think so, honey."

Not Steve. Using Steve's voice. Playing with it. Learning from it. Getting used to it.

More grunting and squealing. It wasn't like a pig, not exactly. But that was the closest frame of reference she had for the sound. It was larger than that. Deeper than that. And there was a slight human quality to it as well, almost like a man pretending to be a pig.

More stamping of feet on the soil. Heavy thuds that brought to her mind the image of large hooves. The sound picked up its pace and traveled to the side of the room where the window was uncovered. The sensor light Steve had set up in a tree to try and scare away deer and boars went off. It was directly outside that window.

Lucy ran to the wall and turned off the lights. Jacob stood frozen in the middle of the room. She grabbed his hand and pulled him with her out of view of the window. She ran through her mind if there was anything in the room she could use as a weapon. Aside from the tall lamp in the corner where they hid, there was nothing.

Something hard struck the wall beneath the window. It rattled the glass. Again, and again the sound came. Each one a little louder, a little nearer. The sensor light stayed on, flooding the room with a ghostly white light. She and Jacob crouched down to the floor, her shoulder leaning against the wall. The grunting came in even louder now. She felt

He heard a low grumbling coming from outside. It grew in intensity until he realized it was the engine of a car.

This late at night?

He thought about that American family that moved in down the road. They would be the only ones near enough, or having any cause to, drive up here this late at night.

Well, if they didn't mess with the skulls I've been putting up, they should be fine. Besides, it's been decades since it has shown up. I'm sure there's nothing to worry about.

Headlights broke into his cluttered home from his dirty window-panes. Makoto hobbled toward his front door and he heard a car door open and shut, but the headlights stayed on.

Before he could open his door, a frantic pounding assaulted it.

"Please, open up! Help!"

Makoto didn't understand the words, but he understood the tone. He knew he could breathe a sigh of relief. Before he turned the handle, he froze. It had always spoken to Makoto in the voice of his mother and sometimes of his little sister. Both of whom had vanished into the woods. He hadn't given thought to whether or not it could speak in other languages.

Makoto laughed. His deer skull was nailed to the wall right by the front door. He had dozens more outside. The rules were obeyed, so he should be safe.

Then why are my hands shaking?

The door shook with the pounding and the voice of the young man came through, pleading in desperation.

Fuck it, if I die, I die.

Makoto opened the door.

A boy collapsed into his arms, nearly knocking him over.

"Jay-Cobe, what's wrong?"

The boy looked at him with wet and red eyes and began speaking fast. So many words and none of them that he knew. But he knew what must have happened. He shut the door and led the boy into the living room. He sat him down in his oversized recliner, which the boy made look like it belonged to a child.

"Stay here, Jay-Cobe."

Makoto walked into his bedroom and grabbed a machete from off the wall where he hung all his tools. It was next to a chainsaw, a bear trap, razor wire, and several sledgehammers. He walked back into the living room. The boy looked up at him with wide eyes and raised his hands as if the old man was going to bring the blade down on his head. Makoto ignored him, shuffled to the front door, opened it, and walked outside.

Crickets chirped and a breeze shook the tree branches in the forest. Makoto looked back at his front door to make sure the skull was still fastened to it. It was. As were the other dozen skulls he could see posted on sticks along the border to his property.

"Jacob, honey, where are you?"

The woman's voice came from the darkness just outside the border of bones. The words were unintelligible to him, but he knew it must be the boy's mother. He heard the boy yell something from inside the home as he shut the door, leaving Makoto outside.

That's fine.

The bushes in front of him, blanketed under the cover of night, shifted as something large made its way closer to the border. Pig squeals and grunting. He knew what the wild boar in the area sounded like and this was not it. He knew the heavy breathing and the excited jabbering *it* made with its large and hungry mouth. Years had passed since last he heard it and now all the animal fear and buried memories came back to him.

The thing made a low moan and adjusted its words. Slipping from English to crude Japanese and back again, as if it was out of practice.

"Makoto, time for dinner."

Came his mother's voice.

"You always cheat."

Came his sister's.

He gripped the machete handle tighter. He knew it was useless against the thing in the woods. Being near seventy years old, Makoto thought he was done with it. He thought he could just slip away into a peaceful death, beer in hand, fly fishing lulling to an eternal sleep. Fear pierced his chest, and his heart skipped several beats, causing him to get lightheaded and nearly fall over. If he was to go this way, meeting the jaws of the nameless terror in the trees, then maybe it could redeem a lifetime of regret. Of how he stood there in the field, watching it drag his sister away by her hair, caught between its teeth. Of crying in a corner as it broke the window and took his mother. Of how his father slowly deteriorated into a husk of a man, doing himself in with a rope around the neck.

If he could save one person, maybe his life could mean something more than the slow motion of slipping away into the grave.

A shadow came near the border. His outdoor floodlights, attached to his roof, created a pool of light that extended a foot or so past the deer skull post in front of him. The shadow moved right next to the line between light and dark. Its flaming eyes seethed with hunger. He could see the hulking mass in the dark, rising far above him.

It took a step into the light. Something clothed in tattered rags like unraveled blood-stained bandages. A face with four fangs, two on the upper jaw and two on the lower. A face as big as a man. With two hooved feet.

"Makoto, time for dinner."

He braced himself.

Blue and red lights flashed over the ramshackle home and yard. They lit up the cavernous eyes of the skulls, giving them a psychedelic appearance of life. The patrol car drove up the driveway and pulled over next to a Jeep, driver door open and headlights still on. The cop car's headlights lit up an elderly man on his knees in the yard, holding a machete. There was a black stain on it.

The officers jumped out of the vehicle and took out their Nambu revolvers and pointed it at the man.

"Drop the blade!" One of them shouted at the man. He did so and it was lost in the grass by his knees.

The officers approached him cautiously, asking his name and what he was doing out in the dark with the weapon. They asked him if he knew about the house down the street and why their registered vehicle was at his house.

He didn't look at the officers. Hardly registered their presence. All he could say was, "It didn't want me. The skulls are useless if you touch the tree."

One officer stayed with the man while his partner went into the home.

The red and blue lights washed over the man's face, revealing the glisten of tears in his eyes. He muttered the same line about skulls and trees while the officer kept a safe distance from him, gun now lowered, but hand on the grip just in case.

The officer looked out in the woods, trees shifting between crimson and azure. Was that a boar out there, running into the woods? Maybe a bear given the size?

"Kimura, come over here," said the officer just now exiting the house.

Kimura walked over to the other officer as he whispered something in his ears. Kimura responded by taking out a pair of cuffs and latching them onto the old man. They lifted him to his feet and led him to the back of their patrol car and shut the door after him. Kimura called into his radio for backup for a possible homicide.

The Johnson family is missing, every door to their home has been smashed in.

Their neighbor Makoto Oda was found outside his home with a machete in his hand and the Johnson family's car in his yard.

No one else found in his home.

Large amounts of blood found all over his living room.

The old man looked out the window of the car into the woods. In the flashes of the lights, a large face stared back at him.

It smiled.

FISH HOOKS

"**H**appy birthday baby," Marie says.

She clutches the crumpled photograph to her face. Closes her eyes and presses the picture against her lips. Tears run down her dirty cheeks and soak into the picture of the boy in a blue soccer jersey.

When she opens her eyes—ringed purple and baggy— the light reflecting off the algae covered pond causes her to wince. For a moment she thinks about letting go of the photograph. To let the wind carry it off into the desert beyond the park she stands in.

Nearby an empty swing set moves in the hot breeze. Brown weeds strangle the slide, wrapping around its steps like a mummified anaconda. Moss entombs the seesaw. There are no children here and maybe that's why she puts the photograph back into her jeans pocket.

Somebody has to remember them.

"Hey Marie, you done? We need to get the harvest back to town soon."

She turns around and sees Jess tapping her foot on the grass with her arms crossed. Her face wears a mask of sternness, but Marie knows it's for show. Her austere demeanor breaks, and she lets free a slight smile that resembles a grimace, almost as if the woman has forgotten how to do it.

"Yeah sorry, I'm coming."

Jess nods her head and walks out of sight.

Marie walks across the overgrown jungle of a park. She climbs over a fallen light post, her feet crunch over the shards hidden in the weeds. Good thing she wears hiking boots everywhere now. Nice ones she found in a military surplus store. Ones with Kevlar shoelaces. She also wears a jacket. And a gun strapped to her waist. And a backpack filled to the brim with water, food, and medical supplies.

Can't be too safe.

When Marie comes out of the park and into the street she sees Jess and Mark lifting burlap sacks into the back of a dirty pickup truck. She joins them and helps get the last of the potatoes into the bed.

"What took you so long?" Mark asks as they lift the last sack. His sunburnt face reflects the anger in his voice.

"Hey leave her alone. You'd want her to do the same for you," Jess says. She looks over at Marie and smiles. A thin, desperate smile. This time it moves beyond the scowl, and she shows her teeth. It unnerves Marie to see this attempt. Like children playing in the park, smiles are a rarity nowadays.

"No, I get it. I lost my wife so of course I fucking get it," Mark says. "We all lost somebody. But it's getting dark soon and she's holding us up. We have to go now."

"Mark," Marie says in a soft tone. "Please."

Her dark eyes, usually sharp and intimidating, today are glossed over and shiny with tears. Mark must have been affected by this because, in a way foreign to the man as learning Chinese, he awkwardly shuts up.

No one talks as Mark drives them back into town. Marie stares out the grimy window across the landscape. Barren. Dry. Mostly bereft of life. Patches of good soil for planting can be found nearest the town. Mostly the hardy stuff; potatoes, corn, squash.

The lifeblood of the town.

The sun pours its fire into the air. Marie licks her cracked lips and her throat screams for water. She takes a single sip, all that's left, from her canteen. She won't take more from her backpack, never know when she'll really need it.

She'll have to wait her turn at the water tower for more.

Tomorrow.

The sun is two hours away from setting.

Not enough time.

The truck rolls into Pleasance. A town once full of retirees sitting in lawn chairs, sipping homemade margaritas, watching the open landscapes and pretending they were free and young. The Sierra Mountains are in the distance, breaking into the blue sky like jagged teeth taking a bite out of it.

Dust clouds fly up as the truck comes to a stop. A group of people are waiting to carry the potatoes into the warehouse. Marie gets out of the car and nods at Jeff, the man nearest her. His weatherworn face, cracked with age and sun, looks mean but his eyes denote kindness. She hands him a bag from the truck, and he sets off towards the warehouse. The others in the group grab the rest of the food and soon the crowd has dispersed like mice running for shelter. Nobody dispenses small talk. Marie used to say she hated talk about the weather or what coworkers thought about the latest episode of Shogun. Now she craves it nearly as much as she does water.

The blood red sun is dipping below the now black hills. The crimson light colors in the drab and lifeless town. The grays and browns now painted red. Dozens of men, women, and children are seen walking briskly back to their homes. Each window boarded shut. Each lawn overgrown and dead. Marie sees Jeff walking back from the warehouse and stopping at a makeshift tower in the town square. There are storm sirens up there, under a canopy of blankets and plywood. Jeff ascends the ladder. He's got watch tonight.

Mark splits away from Jess and Marie. muttering to himself about people not taking things seriously. He doesn't look back at them or say goodnight. Marie feels the rage in the man more than usual. As if residual heat from past trauma radiated off his face.

Marie and Jess make their way to a one storied blue house, shuttered and neglected as all the others. No time to take care of the grass nowadays.

They walk into the house. Marie drops her bags on the sofa, Jess takes hers to her own room down the hall. The light is quickly draining from the room like blood from a arterial wound. They still have electricity in Pleasance thanks to Jeff and a few other guys who used to work various maintenance jobs in the past. Just not at night.

Never at night. Marie takes the picture out of her pocket and places it on the coffee table. She takes off her clothes and changes into sweatpants and a t-shirt. She goes to the fridge and unplugs it. She takes out the cooked meat inside and devours it. She hears the backup generator next door at the Roxy's go silent. Marie finishes her meal, doesn't wash her hands, and moves to the sofa. She has piles of blankets to make it through the cold night. The front door opens, and Owen comes in, looking haggard and skeletal. More than usual anyway.

"Hey," Marie says.

"Hey," he returns. "Your turn tonight yeah?"

"Yep."

He moves down to his room after grabbing his food from the now dead fridge.

Minutes pass and darkness is about to consume the home. Marie grabs the zip ties and heads to Owen's room. He's already passed out, an empty glass bottle of vodka rests near his head like a pillow. Marie ties his hands to the headrest, and he gives no protest.

She moves to Jess' room and finds her in bed as well. Marie goes to tie her hands. Jess offers them.

"Hey," Jess says. Marie can no longer see her face, but she senses the empathy laden in her voice. "Today was rough for you. I'm sorry."

"It's okay, thank you. It'll get better tomorrow."

"Yeah I suppose so. It's always the hardest on birthdays, isn't it? Sure you don't want me to take over tonight?"

Marie says nothing but squeezes Jess' hand before tying them both to the headrest.

"It's good for me to have something to think about. I'm not gettin' sleep anyway."

"Alright. Good night."

Marie returns the words and makes her way in the dark to the living room. She's done this hundreds of times by now and knows the layout by heart.

She goes to the sofa and sits down. Always better to sleep near an exit she figures. Just in case.

She ties one hand to the leg of the sofa. She won't be able to pull the furniture by herself, she knows by experience. She grabs her knife on the table and tosses it a few feet away.

No temptations. It won't last long anyway.

She lays awkwardly on the sofa and waits.

Sleep doesn't find her. Not that she wants it to. Her eyes are fixed on the boarded-up window.

Sometimes they don't come at all. Those nights are almost worse. The never-ending anticipation that finds no release. And as much as she'll never admit to anyone, there's a perverse joy in their visits. She knows its suicide to think this way, but it doesn't change how she feels.

The walls rattle.

A slight tremor at first that quickly picks up into a violent shaking. Marie sits up, one hand hanging off the sofa, bound to it.

Through the boarded-up windows of the house silver lights leak through. As if a great search light were scanning the outside of the home. It lands on her skin. Cold to the touch.

They're here.

The smell of fresh cut grass. Her eyes start to well up. She knows what's coming next.

Then comes the taste of beer and hotdogs. The sound of a crowd cheering. The smell of Javier's vanilla-tinged cologne. Then she sees him. Running across the field in a blue jersey. Stealing the ball from Alejandro. He looks up at her and smiles.

Marie tries to stand up but the zip ties hold her down.

She tries again and almost screams Daniel's name. She wants to. More than anything to wants to speak his name but she knows what happens if she does. She stays silent but her body tries to stand again. Again, the sofa keeps her grounded.

"Mommy look what I can do," Daniel says. He raced across that field and scores a goal. She feels the overwhelming need to cheer him on but stops herself.

The lights pass her and disappear. The rumbling quiets down. Soon the clear image of that soccer field fades into black. She sits back on the sofa.

Exhausted. But they usually don't pass by more than once. She lays down and lets sleep finally take her.

"Holy shit!" Jess' voice explodes from the dark.

Marie is awake now. She bolts up so fast she nearly pulls her shoulder too hard against her restraint.

"Marie, hurry!"

She doesn't understand. It's still dark out. She shouldn't be yelling. They will hear her.

Soon she understands what's happening. She hears the screaming from outside. She hears the sirens blaring. She sees the shadow of something burning through the slats of the windows. She guesses it's a car by the vague shape she can make out.

More screaming.

Somebody fucked up.

She rolls off the sofa, hand still tied to the leg. She grabs her jeans and throws them in the direction she remembers throwing the knife. Usually, she does this lasso trick in daylight, but her jeans find it on the third try. She pulls the knife close. Cuts the zip tie. Puts on her clothes, nearly jumping into her jeans. She crawls down the hall to Jess' room, careful not to draw attention of any kind.

Jess only shouted out once. Enough to alert Marie, hopefully it wasn't one time too much. Marie moves into Jess' room and crawls to the bed.

She stands and cuts the ties off of her wrists. She feels Jess' hands on her face, a caress of gratitude on her cheeks.

Jess whispers, "We need to get Owen."

Marie crawls across the floor towards his room as she hears Jess put her clothes on.

The walls shake.

Without the ties Marie knows they're vulnerable, but they have to move fast. With all the noise outside it's only a matter of time. She pushes Owen's room open. He's still snoring.

The sirens continue as more screams are heard, nearer the house now.

Then come rays of white light through curtains. The shaking gets louder now like the approach of a massive tank.

Marie freezes. She hears Jess shuffle up to her from behind.

The roof of Owen's room comes flying off.

"Move Jess, move," Marie hisses, careful not to raise her voice. Before she turns around, she sees the bright light descending into the room and Owen struggling against his ties, trying to stand and greet it.

The women move down the hall and make their way to the front door. Marie finds her backpack in the dark and puts it on.

"You don't know how long I've wanted to see you again," Owen says. There's joy in his voice. Nearly on the verge of a sob.

Then he is screaming. Shouting and yelling. A wet tearing sound. A splash of liquid on the ground. A loud thud from something heavy being dropped. Most likely the bed.

"I don't have my bag," Jess says, panic shattering her quiet voice.

"Doesn't matter, we need to go now."

Marie opens the front door and Jess follows her outside.

Chaos.

People are running down the streets. The house across the street has been flattened entirely. Someone is running towards Marie, shouting as he flees.

"Run!" He shouts.

A light appears above him. A white flame the size of a person. It lights up the man and Marie sees that its Jeff. For a moment he looks at Marie with mouth hung open and terror in his face. Then he looks upwards at the light and lifts his hands to it.

"Marie, he's gone we need to go!"

Jess grabs her hand and pulls her away. Before Marie turns, she sees Jeff fly up into the sky. The lights goes out.

They turn and flee. Marie hears Jeff's final cries. Pleading for mercy.

Then silence.

They climb over a backyard fence and run across the dark yard. They keep going until they hit the hedges. There's a small hole, big enough for a person to fit through. Marie and Jess and Owen have practiced this before.

Just in case.

They edged their way inside and, once fully hidden, they embrace each other and wait.

The sirens cut out. Followed by metal crashing. The screams are getting fewer and far between now.

Marie tells herself that most people had to have gotten out. She knows this is a lie.

A light rises from behind the house they are facing. It shines its chilling light across the lawn.

Marie feels the pull of the fresh cut grass. The shouts and the food. Javier so close to her she feels the warmth of his body.

And then there's Daniel. Smiling at her. She feels herself start to stand. If it wasn't for Jess holding onto her she would have. She feels Jess' nails dig into her arm and she snaps out of the dream. Jess is being similarly affected. Marie holds her down. The roof of the home is broken open by an unseen force. Like someone cracking open a crab and pulling out the flesh, the light descends into the home, the walls bulge until they shatter, one of them falls to the ground, a woman is pulled from the home and flies upward.

She disappears just feet above the home. As if dissolved by the darkness itself. The light floats out of the home and the structure collapses completely. The light goes out.

The women hold each other in the ensuing silence. Hours pass. Neither of them sleep.

The first light of dawn comes as a welcome friend. The Blue Jays that have made their nest in the tree above the hedge begin their morning song. As the dull light appears, the women leave their makeshift shelter.

"Do you think anybody made it?" Marie asks, no longer in a whisper.

"Has to be. But we need to leave. Now."

Marie knows this. Once they come, once they know people are still around, they don't leave until everyone has been taken.

"A truck, Mark's truck," Jess almost blurts out. "We can take it to Oreville."

"No, too risky. If we got hit, they'll be next if they aren't already."

"The cabin?"

"Yeah, it's the only place far enough."

They walk through the wreckage of their home, hoping to find Jess' bag quick. They'll need the water more than anything. After a few minutes they quit. Sunset is still far off, but time has a way of catching you off guard. They walk down the street and turn left on Pine Avenue. Soon they come to the square and see the mangled corpse of the watch tower. Marie imagines Jeff keeping watch, seeing the lights breaking into homes and sounding the alarm. He could have stayed quiet, or moved out unseen, but he sounded the alarm and died for it.

Most of the homes have been smashed. A few are left standing, but Marie knows this will not be the case tomorrow. Her home for the past nine months is gone. Time to start over.

Again.

They make their way to where the cars are kept. The ones with gas that is. They see a truck and run over to it. The keys are usually kept in the ignition for each vehicle but when they come to the it they see none. Marie looks down at the tires.

Slashed.

Every car.

Mark's truck is missing.

"Holy fuck," Jess says. "Somebody did this on purpose."

"Who could be so stupid?"

The lights never broke routine. If you tied yourself down, stayed quiet, and stayed hidden, they always passed.

"Did," Marie starts and chews her lip. "Did somebody want them here? To kill everyone?"

They don't say it but the missing truck confirms it in their minds.

Jess screams and kicks the side of the truck. She regrets her decision immediately and falls down holding her foot.

Marie puts her hand on Jess' shoulder. "We have to move."

"Where?" Jess shouts.

Marie knows there is nowhere to go.

"Maybe, they'll come back here tonight looking for people. We might be able to walk to the hills without them noticing us."

Jess miles. She agrees. Marie knows she's lying for her sake. But what else can they do?

Marie helps her up and they make for the warehouse. If they're going to hike, they'll need supplies.

They see no one as they walk. If just yesterday Pleasance was a husk of what used to be, today it was a sarcophagus.

They pass the ruins of homes. Trails of blood splashed across the pavement. A pink tricycle resting up in a tree. Marie can't bear to look.

Soon they come to the warehouse. A semi-cylindrical building full of food, medical supplies, water.

The front doors are open.

"Okay, I'll grab some water and food," Marie says. "You'll need to find a bag, probably one by the batteries. Grab some of those and a flashlight and radio if you can."

"Roger that."

Jess is a few steps ahead of Marie.

A light burns in the darkness of the warehouse. Jess is two or three steps ahead of Marie and nearest the opening. As they get close Marie is hit with the smell of fresh cut grass.

She pauses a moment. It's day out, this shouldn't be happening.

"Jess, stop."

She's too late. Jess is walking closer to the opening; hands are lifting up out in front of her. A light comes to life from within the dark warehouse.

"Jess!" Marie runs forward and wraps her arms around Jess' waist.

Then comes the voice.

"Mommy, look at what I can do."

They're too close.

She releases Jess and walks in line behind her. To shuffle towards the white light in the dark. Marie can see the soccer field overlap the black void of the warehouse.

Jess speaks. "Tommy. I love you so much."

They enter the building. The light hovers above Jess. She looks up and raises her hands.

For a moment the spell is broken as Marie sees something dark shift ahead. Something black and snakelike wraps around Jess' feet. Then she is ripped upwards as if caught in a hunter's trap. The light disappears. And in that moment Marie is free from its pull. But she's too late. Jess screams. She shouts, "Marie, run!"

Marie has never been this close to the lights before. And now she sees it. Before the light extinguished itself, she saw some limb hanging out from a larger black mass. Like the stalk of an angler fish. Jess's screams are cut short by the shredding sound of something wet.

Marie turns and sprints out of the building. She runs to a safe distance and keeps on running.

She never looks back.

Hours have passed. Marie walks through the desert, staring down at her feet. She tells herself that to cry is to deplete her body's water supply. That helps her to not think about what happened. She looks up at the hills, still far off. She guesses it will take her until tomorrow to reach them. She'll have to spend the night out here. Exposed.

Soon she passes a billboard. Bleached by the sun. It might be a hotel advertisement, she can't tell. She reaches the summit of a small hill and sees a town in front of her. Roseville. Uninhabited as far as she knows. And halfway to the mountains and the cabin. She looks at the sun. Soon it will be a memory. This will have to do for now.

She walks into the town. The buildings still stand. That's a good sign. Marie turns a corner and sees a motel. In the parking lot, Mark's truck.

Rage boils in her bones. She could leave and forget what she saw. That would be the smart move. Then she feels Jess' hands in hers. She sees Jeff's scared eyes.

She doesn't know what she will do but she can't just walk away. The tiniest spark of hope exists, that this is a misunderstanding. Just talk to him first.

But somebody slashed those tires. Somebody brought them last night.

Her plans to sneak up on Mark are soon dashed.

From behind her, "Marie?"

Shaking with rage and fear she turns around.

As something comes flying across the side of her skull.

She's awake. Head is splitting in pain. The urge to vomit rises in her throat. She batters her eyes open and sees nothing.

Am I dead? Floating in limbo?

No. A red glow comes to life from somewhere behind her. The electric buzz of a light hums on and off, on and off.

Then terror seizes her. It's night. She's outside. And there's a light on nearby.

"Don't worry Marie, it'll be over soon," Mark says as he comes into view and sits down on the pavement in front of her. He's holding a bat. She notices his truck to her right. She's in the parking lot still.

"Why?" She asks, her voice barely able to make itself known.

"Violet."

"What?" Marie starts to get off the ground. Mark lets her but bounces the bat in his hand.

"I need to see her again."

"Mark," Marie says and grabs the side of head. She looks at her hand. Red. "They're not really there. It's all a trick."

"I don't care."

Marie almost lets another question pass her lips but stalls. "You did something to make them come last night didn't you?"

Mark nods.

"To...to see your wife again? To use our friends like lures to bring more of them so you could see her longer?"

"Smart bitch."

Marie can hardly comprehend this. "If you want that so bad why not just let them take you?"

"I know what that means. That means I get dead. But if I have someone, like you, then I can sit back and have her all to myself again."

There's no reasoning here. Marie turns to run and falls. She didn't even notice it. The rope tied around her ankles, connected to a cement pole a few feet away.

"If they take me, they'll look for you right after," she screams at him.

He doesn't bother to answer. He gives her one last look. She can almost feel regret in his green eyes. Regret and loss. Loss so great she's convinced he won't stop this. He'll hop around where he can to get his fix, no matter how many lives he puts at risk. Mark enters a motel room nearby on the first floor. He'll have to be close to feel the effects of the lights.

Marie turns to the rope and brings it to her teeth. She gnaws at it like a rabid rodent. Maybe she can chew through it by morning. But with the motel sign blazing in the dark, she knows they won't be long in coming.

Then she remembers. Mark has taken her knife and her backpack. But he has left her boots on. Boots with Kevlar shoestrings. She undoes her laces from one shoe. She feeds the lace between the rope and her skin. she holds both ends of the lace and starts a sawing motion. At first the pain on her ankle is slight but it quickly turns to fire. The laces are cutting through the rope with ease. And her skin. And her palms. But she saws through the rope in less than a minute. She knows her hands and ankle are bleeding, but she doesn't have time for that. She gets up and runs. A door opens and slams behind her.

"Get back here you bitch."

She sprints towards the desert, but Mark's footsteps quickly overtake. He tackles her to the ground. Her face slams into the pavement. He tries lifting her up but she kicks and shouts and then bites his hands.

He lets go of her, "Fuck!"

She falls down on her back. He's on her instantly, bat to her throat. He's pinning her into the road.

"I just wanted to see her again. You're not keeping me from her."

She feels her throat collapsing under the bat. Her feet kick out at nothing.

Then they are both bathed in light. Mark loosens his grip on the bat and stands to his feet. Above them a burning white light.

Mark lifts his hands and cries out, "Babe! I need you!"

A dark tentacle wraps around his waist. "I love you so much."

It lifts him into the sky and the light goes out. Marie sees it in that moment before the light dies, like a flash photograph revealing for just a second what was hidden in the room. She saw teeth. She saw milky eyes. She saw a floating mass, hovering, swimming through the air. She saw Mark held before its face.

In the dark she now hears him scream until she doesn't.

Something rains down on her. But she knows there's not a cloud in sight. She scrambles away, gets to her feet, and runs. She sees more lights, dozens of them, swimming through the ghost town. She leaves them all as she races into the open plains. Panting, heart beating out of her chest, she makes it to a hill. Gasping for breath she turns around and sees the lights far off, still in town, not pursuing.

It's almost beautiful. Like moving stars here on earth. She takes out her photograph of Daniel. Unable to see it clearly in the dark but that's alright. Just to feel it one last time. She kisses it, holds it out to the wind, and lets go. Pain crackles in her heart, almost as bad as the wound on her hands and leg. But it's a freeing sort of pain.

She turns to leave into the wilderness and is hit with scent of fresh cut grass. It's not a dark desert before her, no, it's a soccer field as clear as day. Daniel is right there, waving at her. She's never been this close before.

"Mommy look at what I can do."

"Yes," she says. "I will."

She walks to him across the sun kissed field. She feels the morning dew brush against her ankles, now pain free. Daniel opens his arms, and she rushes to him. She holds him tight. Her breath is taken away by the force of her hug.

"I'm never leaving you again baby."

Daniel wraps his arms around her waist.

Funny.

His hands are colder than she thought they'd be.

Longer.

Stronger.

SMILE WIDE FOR ME

R ina held the photograph with her fingertips as if it was just
dragged out of the sewer and dripping with chunky brown liquid. She couldn't take her eyes off it. She couldn't drop it. It clung to her
hands like a bad dream right after waking.

Her breathing quickened. The fingertips holding the top edges of the
Polaroid went numb.

She was looking at a photograph of herself. Sleeping in her bed. Her
body under the covers, head exposed, all lit up in a harsh white light.

She looked so pale and ghost-like in the picture. Her black hair further
highlighted the sickly pallor her skin took on in that light.

Her lips quivered and her stomach felt like it was rising to her throat.

Whoever took this picture did it with the flash on. Why didn't she
wake up? Never mind the floorboards that must have squeaked and her
neighbor's dog out in their yard that must have barked. Why didn't she
wake up to the flash? It was a harsh light that must have been accompa-
nied by the sound of the camera taking the shot.

She let go of the photo and it fell onto her cluttered desk. The sound
of phones being answered and the clicks and clacks of keyboards sent her

head reeling. She felt constricted. Like she was trapped in a straitjacket. She needed air. Now.

Rina placed a notebook over the photo, stood up, and with head down, nearly sprinted through the office.

Picture of me?

Why?

The flash.

Didn't wake up.

He was in my room.

What does he want?

The flash.

It can't be him.

Not after so long.

Suddenly papers were flying, and she was falling backward on her ass. "What the hell!?"

She propped herself up on her elbows and saw her boss, Mr. Mills. He was on the ground, covered in paperwork-soaked coffee. The mug now lay shattered on the ground.

"Oh my God, I'm so sorry." She crawled on her hands and knees, picking up the papers, and offered them to Mr. Mills, who was now standing back up.

He snatched the papers from her and sighed. "Rina, in my office."

He walked away, brushing his hand in vain at a large coffee stain on his white button-up shirt. He entered his office and stood holding the door open. Rina followed in.

"Sit."

She did.

Mr. Mills waddled over to his desk and sat on the edge of it like a high school Lit. teacher trying too hard to be cool. He leaned forward and put his hands on his knees.

"Where has yer mind been, girl?" Being called "girl" instantly transported her back to being chewed out by her father for coming home late as a teen. All her boss needed was a pair of furry sideburns and he'd be giving her father a run for his money. "Yer performance has been lackin' for weeks. Yer team says you've been missin' meetins' and deadlines. And now you plow me over like I'm a corn field ready for plantin'." Another trait Mr. Mills shared with dear ol' dad, corny corn jokes.

"I'm sorry, I just haven't been getting enough sleep lately."

"Yer what, twenty-five years old now?"

A flicker of light to her left, outside the office window, caught her attention. Almost like a flash.

"Thirty."

His jaw hung loose in actual astonishment. "Shit girl, ol' nuff ya' ought to be home carin' for some lil ones by now. And can't get yerself enough sleep she says. I'll tell ya' what," he said as he tried to swing his body off the desk. He failed the first time and needed a second swing of his legs to get his body off the edge. "I'll give ya' one more week. Can't handle yer 'sponsibilities by then, yer out."

"I swear it won't happen again. I'll do my best—"

He waved his hand like a swarm of flies were flying out of her mouth.

"Don't need yer swearin' more than I need a fuckin' doctor tellin' me what ta' eat. I know MickeyDee's will kill me, and I don't care. What I don' know is if you can do the job."

He opened the door for her and didn't even wait for her acknowledgment. Rina rose from her chair and left the office. A *whoosh* of air hit her backside and ballooned her blouse as the door slammed shut behind her. She walked back to her desk, head held low and focused on the ugly brown carpet. At least she wasn't running this time and didn't have to worry about crashing into someone.

She resumed her seat at her desk. One week to get her act together? She didn't mind losing the job so much, she always had enough in savings to fall back on. It was the embarrassment of failure that made it a tough pill to swallow.

There was nothing Rina Sagawa hated more than to be humiliated.

But why was she so tired? The past week had come out of nowhere. Every morning she woke up exhausted. Once she brewed a pot of coffee without actually adding in the coffee. A mug of hot water wasn't exactly the best way to start off a Monday. The forty-minute commute was especially dangerous. At least in the morning she had the light of day to keep her awake. Her head dipped down and bowed to tiredness while she drove home in the dark.

She even drove by an accident just yesterday. White minivan bisected by a concrete divider. Shards of glass took up the reflection of the cop lights, refracting their luminosity across the blood on the pavement. If she wasn't careful, that could be her.

The photograph.

She saw a corner of the picture sticking out from under the notebook. It revealed a white light highlighting the foot of her bed.

Is this why I've been tired? Has this been happening the whole week? Messing with my sleep?

She pulled the photo out and crumpled it in her palm. She put the balled-up thing into her purse and zipped it up. Rina wouldn't be going to the police with this. She had a feeling she knew exactly who was doing it and if it was anything like last time, cops would be useless. This was something she needed to solve. Quickly.

And fuck this job and fuck Mr. Mills. He can go suck on some corn and cry about it.

Rina packed up her things and left. She could feel the eyes of Mr. Mills peering out from in between the blinds of his office window as she stomped her way out of there. This wasn't quitting, but if he wanted to take it as such, well, go on then.

She entered the elevator and punched the button for the garage on the top floor. Waiting for the doors to close she saw Mr. Mills' head leaning out of his doorway, staring at her. Right before the doors shut, she flipped her middle finger at him.

She smiled, imagining his expression, his face turning cherry red and sweaty. The doors opened and she walked out. Her heels clacked on the cement; echoes shot out into the empty garage. They gave her the impression that somebody else was walking around in some unseen corner. The garage was full of the slightly sweet smell of gasoline. She wrapped her arms around her shoulders and shivered. She took out her keys from her purse and pressed the unlock button. She heard the click and saw the red lights flash from her blue Honda CR-V. The combo of colors reminded her of the accident from yesterday. Red and blue lights splashing over the freeway.

Rina recognized the van. The driver had cut her off exactly one week before deciding to cut herself in half, legs somewhere in the bottom of the crushed van, upper torso hanging out a window.

She shook the images away, opened her car door, and got inside. Shut the door. Put on her seatbelt—safety first— and started the engine.

And then she saw it.

Wedged into the visor overhead, another photograph. She spun around in her seat but saw no one else in the car. Turning back around, she ripped the photo from the visor. Not one but two pictures together.

One was a picture of her, bathed in the white light of a flash as if it were taken in a dark room. It was in Mr. Mills' office. In the day. Him sitting on the desk's edge, leaning forward. The second, again, had the same washed-out flash effect. It showed her in her car, twisting around and looking into the back seat. Wearing the same white blouse she had on now.

Rina ripped both of them to pieces and tossed them out the window. She drove out of the garage.

On her way home she passed a bridge with a cement divider between the lanes. There was some shattered glass on the road and faint stains that were a light brown against the asphalt.

She slowed down, took out her phone, and took a picture.

Kyle was a nice man. A little too talkative for Rina with a habit of picking at his teeth with his fingers, but cute enough to stomach his ramblings. Whatever his faults, he provided a distraction for the night. A relief from going home. For now, at least.

"So, you quit?" He said between shoving a buttered roll into his mouth and then chewing it by moving his lower jaw too much, like a horse.

"Yeah, not exactly, but I wouldn't be surprised if I'm fired. But you know what? It felt good to let that bastard know what I think of him."

"Shit." He commented poignantly before attacking the next and last roll.

Rina stared at him in horror as the bits of bread and streams of butter oozed down his chin. She glanced around their table. A dozen or so people sat at tables with white cloths draped over them. Candles lit. Waiters stalking around wearing bow ties. Extreme embarrassment washed over her.

There was only one way she knew for how to deal with that.

"What you gonna do now?" He asked.

"Don't know. I was thinking maybe I should start traveling. Time to get out and see new things, you know? It's been too long not being myself."

"Cool, I've always wanted to go to Thailand." He smiled. If there was ever a time to engage in his tooth picking it should have been now. A piece of spinach was lodged between his upper front two teeth.

"About that," she started, "I think we should—"

"Hold that thought, babe, I need to hit the can."

He rose and walked over to the men's bathroom.

"—see other people." She sighed.

Kyle was a distraction, yes. But at what cost?

She thought of her ex, Rob, as she twirled spaghetti around her fork. They had been happy once. Like her and Kyle. Until Rob ran away with her best friend, Christine. She found out on her birthday of all days. A casual glance at his phone brought her world tumbling down. Since then, she learned to let him go and be herself. Or at least she tried. Maybe it was time to do the same with Kyle? Let him go.

I know how.

She checked her watch. Kyle had been gone now ten minutes. She texted him to see if he was okay.

He responded immediately: *What the fuck? I don't know how you did that, but seriously messed up. Going home now. Need time to think.*

What are you talking about?

The picture in the urinal!!

Rina looked up from the phone and scanned the restaurant. Above the ambient chatter of the people, she thought she heard a camera zoom.

What picture?

This one!!!!

A few seconds later it popped up on her chat. A picture of her and Kyle sitting at the table, this table, him shoving the last roll into his mouth. His eyes were crossed out with red ink and he had a noose drawn in the same color around his neck. He sent another one; it showed him sleeping in his bed, ringed in the light of the flash. A hand with black painted nails, the rest of the person off camera, held out a knife over Kyle's sleeping body.

Rina gripped her phone until her hands hurt and got up to leave.

No dog barking. No floorboards squeaking. The house was still and silent. Doors locked. Windows bolted shut.

She knew it wouldn't make a difference. It never did.

It's been five years and nothing. Why all of a sudden?

Rina sat on her sofa, circled in golden light from a single lamp to her left, darkness everywhere else.. An opened cardboard box on the coffee table sat in front of her. She thumbed through a set of photographs, chucking them into the box when done. Her sister's daughter on her eighth birthday, standing over a chocolate cake with the widest grin imaginable.

A bay at sunset, pink rays of light stretching over dark blue waters. A single beam from the water of a fishing boat. A spec of light in the faded darkness of the photo.

One last picture of a young man with scraggly black hair. A smile that beat all the odds and eyes that saw further than most people could dream. He had his arm slung over a pretty girl in a pink dress.

Red marker had slashed out her eyes years ago.

Rina kissed and caressed the man's face with her lips. Then she put the photos back into the box. Lifted and carried it back into the closet. Put it behind the false board on the wall. Safe and sound.

She walked to the kitchen, flipped on a light over the stove, and brewed another pot of coffee.

No sleep means no more pictures. Well, that's what worked last time. Today was new. New kinds of photos. All in broad daylight. In real-time.

But it will end. It ended last time; it will end this time too.

She grinded the beans in the top of the coffee machine. Poured in the water. Hit the start button so hard she moved the machine back.

Flash.

The blinding light lit up the kitchen for just a moment and then it was gone. In that brief time, it had succeeded in draining all the warmth from her body. Black spots floated over her vision, and it took a few seconds to regain her usual sight. She didn't want to turn around and face the open plan apartment. Anything could be standing there.

Anyone.

Him.

"Please, just leave me alone."

Aside from her intensified breathing, all was silence.

She waited until the coffee was done, poured a mug, straight and black, and took a swig.

No sleep means no more pictures.

She turned around. The stove light and the lamp by the sofa created two pools of relief. The corners of the apartment were painted in deep shadows. She calmly walked over to the sofa and sat down. On the coffee table. Another photograph, turned upside down. She held onto the coffee mug with both hands. A vain attempt to regain some warmth in her blood. By the time she gained the courage to look at the photo, her mug had grown lukewarm.

She put the coffee down. With a shaking right hand, something that reminded her of yesterday's accident. A woman's upper half lying halfway out the passenger window. Glass embedded in the back of her head. Face turned away. An arm that hung limp, swaying like grass in the wind. The other shaking frenetically. A false appearance of life. It was just the nerves; she knew by experience. Rina turned the photo over.

It was her, making coffee in the kitchen.

"It's not my fault. It was your fault. Please stop."

The light in the kitchen burst. Rina screamed and fell off the sofa. The lamp's bulb exploded. The fading glow of the light's filaments silhouetted the figure of a man standing in her kitchen. A shorter woman was next to him. Then it went dark.

A winding sound. The mechanical zoom sound of a camera trying to focus. Rina stood on shaking legs and tried to bury herself in the wall.

Flash.

Blinding light.

"Stop it."

Footsteps leading away from the kitchen and moving into the hall by her bedroom.

Flash.

"Please, stop it!"

The sound of someone running from the hall right into the living room. Right in front of her.

Winding up.

Lens focusing.

Flash.

"You motherfuckers, stop it!" Rina sobbed and began to choke on her tears.

A voice of a man. Not more than two feet in front of her. "Smile wide for me."

Rina's head grew light and she almost fainted.

Flash.

She fell back against the wall and slid down to a sitting position. Buried her face in her hands.

No more voices. No more flashes. She stayed sitting in that spot until the sun poked its way through her curtains. Only then did her muscles relax and did she dare to stand up. In the cool pale light filling her living room she saw it. A pile of photographs on the coffee table. Photographs on the sofa. Pinned to the walls. To the ceiling. The same faces over and over again.

She moved slowly as if the carpet were quicksand. Stress had evaporated any emotion in her. She sat down on the floor in front of the table. Picked up the pictures and shuffled through them.

A woman with short, curly, brown hair. Dressed in a pinstripe suit. Driving a white minivan while talking to someone on the phone.

A pair of tiny hands, nails painted black, holding a brake cable. The other hand holding the wire cutter.

The van smashed into the concrete divider. The woman's twitching hand, still as death in the photograph, hanging out the window.

Rina threw these pictures on the floor.

She went through the rest.

The young handsome man with the black hair. He was asleep in his bed, next to a woman in a pink nightgown. Rob and Christine. White light from a flash enveloped them as they slept.

The next showed the woman's eyes. Not marked out with pen. But gouged out with a knife. The blade buried deep into her right socket so that it couldn't be seen.

The next photo was of the man. Naked. Bound to the bed with razor wire. A look of abject terror on his face.

Next was the same man. No longer afraid. No longer anything. A rope around his neck. Eyes bulging and red. Blood forming around the rope marks.

The last was a photo of Rina. Not tucked under the covers under the white light. Instead, straddling the bodies on the bed. Camera in her hand and turned towards her face. Smile glistening in the harsh flash. Specs of blood on her cheeks and teeth.

She remembered what she said before she took that last picture of each of them. Of everyone she took a photo of.

Before she stabbed out Christine's eyes and strangled Rob and not only cut that bitch in the van's brakes, but also ran her off the road.

Smile wide for me.

Rina ripped each photograph into pieces. Screaming as her black painted nails dug into the sheets and tore them into ribbons. She scattered the pieces all over the living room. Like candy from a piñata.

"Why won't you leave me alone!? Why won't you just stay dead!?"

She ran across the living room, grabbed her keys by the front door, and raced into her car.

She hit the ignition and drove the car out of the drive. She accelerated the gas and flew out of the *cul-de-sac* as if on fire and racing for a nearby stream to douse her head in. The car blasted past the stop sign and she careened right onto Martin Lane going eighty miles an hour.

The winding of a camera. The zooming focus of the lens.

From the backseat.

Flash.

The light reflected off the rearview mirror and blinded her. The car swerved into the oncoming traffic lane. She turned the wheel left and slammed the brakes. They didn't feel like listening to her. She slammed her foot into the brakes again and again, but no response. In a second that felt like a lifetime, she saw the car fly into the concrete divider. Saw the airbag balloon towards her chest. Saw the metal and the glass rain down on her. Saw the twitching hand of the woman in the passenger seat, holding a camera, smiling through shattered teeth.

Before her body and the car became one, Rina heard her say, "Smile wide for me."

DAUGHTER OF SPRING

"Please, please don't leave me. I miss you so much."

Brian Dougherty wept as he stood at the edge of the forest, feet planted on the path that cut through the middle of it. The leafless branches of the birch trees spidered their way across the gray and cloudy sky. They extended from the thick forest and reached over the path itself. Their skinny twigs hung down like fingers, as if to take hold of him.

He looked out into the woods. The trees grew several feet apart from one another with no high grass between them. The forest stretched on for miles, but he could easily walk inside. Walk in and search. Maybe even find her. Even if it took a lifetime and then some.

"Please come back to me. I can't do this without you."

Deep in the forest, just out of range of clear sight, he could see something move. A deer perhaps. Maybe that was its head turned towards him as if listening to his words.

Nearby a black German Shepherd with a red collar was sniffing at the grass without a leash, just off the path. Raising his leg and trying to pee on as many bushes as possible, even though he ran out of urine at least twenty minutes ago.

Brian wiped a hand across his eyes and put them back in his jacket pockets. His breath came out in clouds and rose into the silent air before dissipating and melding with the cold and dreary day.

"Come on, Turtle, best be going."

The dog perked his ears up like satellites and bounced over to Brian's side. Tongue hanging loose. Panting and baring his teeth in a smile, or so Brian thought.

Strange, we like to think dogs smile. Are they? Is that just what we want them to be doing? Guess it's easier that way. Imagine something happy even if it's not true.

Brian walked down the dirt path on autopilot. His feet knew where to go. What rocks to avoid and what branches of the path to take. Turtle ran down the trail. Tail erect. Sniffing to his heart's content.

The trees would never look the same to Brian. He hadn't been out here for three months. Not since the leaves were green and the sun spilled light between the branches. Not since the trail was warm and Cora walked beside him. That was a time when laughter filled the air instead of this damnable silence.

He could almost see her now as she was then.

"I could do this forever," Cora had said as she tossed the tennis ball near the tree line. Turtle raced after it as if it were the last ball in existence.

"Yeah?" Brian asked. Reclining against a willow tree, its leaves flowing over his head and singing like the waves of the ocean. With pen in hand, he was sketching Cora's figure against the birches.

Turtle ran back to Cora and spit out the ball in front of her sandaled feet. He sat down and lifted his front paws towards her and gave a soft whimper, something he only did for Cora. Their special thing. She picked up the ball and chucked it back into the woods.

"Yeah. It's a perfect day. Just coming out here and being able to do this. I'll never get bored."

She smiled as if embarrassed at sounding so innocent and child-like. That was one of the things that Brian loved about her. Smart and serious about life, but in these simple moments she seemed so vulnerable to him. So beautiful. He loved her. He *still* loves her.

Brian dropped his sketch pad, stood up, and walked over to her. Put his arm around her waist and kissed her cheek.

"Good. If you're not bored, I'm not bored."

She pushed him away and laughed. "Dude, get a life."

Turtle ran into Brian's legs, nearly knocking him over. He laughed and tussled the dog's fur and pushed his head around.

That day was perfect. So perfect Brian decided it was time. Do it then and there.

He dug into his pocket and took something out, hidden in his palm.

"What's that?" Cora asked. Still smiling, but she squinted her eyes at him.

He got down on one knee.

She said "yes," of course. He picked her up and twirled her around. Turtle nipping at her flying heels. It's never the good times when time slows down though, is it? On days like these, it speeds up and leaves us behind before we even realize what we had.

She died two weeks after he proposed to her. Nothing dramatic. He almost wished it was something prolonged like cancer, that way he could say goodbye. Fuck, even a car crash would make more sense to him. Cause and effect and all. One day, she stood up from the table after breakfast to grab more coffee. Collapsed without a word. Intracerebral hemorrhage was the word for it. She died before they even made it to the hospital.

Senseless. Unfair. Nothing anyone could do about it.

Brian's eyes stung again with the threat of tears. He called Turtle over to him and shuffled his fur around. Some warmth. Some connection to ease the pain. He slapped the dog's back, and Turtle ran back down the path. Brian followed and they came to the end of the trail which fed out into Meadow Crest Road. He latched the leash back onto Turtle's collar.

"Brian."

He turned back to the forest. His name. That simple greeting. That soft voice he knew better than his own. It dug a hole out of his despair to the surface where there was light. Despite all reason screaming to the contrary, he smiled.

There was no one on the trail. Just the lengthening shadows of the birches closing up the last sliver of pale daylight across the path.

That hurt worst of all. More than her sudden death. More than the weeks that passed by in a numbed haze of sensation. That one word—Brian—it gave him hope. Stupid hope. Now that was gone. He never felt so alone.

Turtle whimpered and pressed up against Brian's legs.

He sat on his hind legs and pawed at the air.

Brian finished washing the dishes. Easy when it was just him. And what some mean by dishes was actually just one glass splattered with beer. The paper plate and plastic fork used to attack the ready-made pasta went straight to the bin. He shut off the news. Something about an election that left the world on fire. He didn't know who the candidates were. Didn't care.

He looked at Cora's Ficus tree by the backyard glass door. Its leaves fell off a few weeks ago and Brian thought it might be dying. He had no clue how to care for plants, that was her thing. He thought about tossing it into the fire soon.

Turtle had curled up on his bed in the corner of the living room and fallen asleep some time ago. His soft snoring made the silence of the home at least somewhat bearable.

He heard the wind outside, flowing through the leaves of fir trees in the backyard. The pine needles rustled together like the clack of tiny feet on a tile floor.

Brian walked by the sofa, not even giving it a glance. Afraid he'd see her sitting there, leaning against a pillow, reading a book. But who was he kidding? He saw her in every room and heard her in every voice. No matter how hard he tried, Cora's essence was infused into every detail of his life. Like a rain-soaked shirt. Brian flipped the lights off, walked up the stairs to his room, and got into bed.

Turtle used to sleep in between him and Cora. Not for months now though. He slept downstairs, night after night, as if waiting for her to come home.

The wind was mellow if not a little loud. It carried his consciousness off, and he started succumbing to sleep.

A creak of wood from downstairs.

Just Turtle.

The metallic sound of his front door locks. His blood ran cold, and he sat up. Turtle didn't make a sound.

Must have been my imagination, otherwise he'd be going crazy right now.

He lowered himself back down, but stayed propped up on his elbows, straining his hearing for any out of place noise. His bedroom door was open, and he could hear Turtle's snoring traveling upstairs.

Time passed and he began falling asleep again.

Another creak and then a squeal from downstairs.

It's just Cora, getting home late from work.

Turtle barked and growled.

Brian shot out of bed, tripped over his sheets, and fell to the floor. He untangled himself, grabbed the baseball bat by the side of his bed, and ran out of the room. Flipped on the hall lights. Ran down the stairs. Hit the lights on the landing.

He ran through the living room with the bat raised over his head, gripped in both hands. Turtle was standing in front of the door—the opened front door—hackles raised and growling. Thick darkness enveloped the doorway, and a cold wind blew inside, fully waking him up. He couldn't see anything outside. Brian ran to the door. Slammed it shut. Locked the deadbolt—*did I forget to do this before bed?*

Brian went from room to room, closet to closet, nook to cranny. He was alone in the house. Turtle stayed by the front door, no longer growling, but pacing back and forth.

Satisfied that no one was in the house, Brian sat down on the downstairs sofa, put the bat on the floor, and called Turtle over to him. The dog walked over, head held low, tail sticking straight out. Brian pet his head and massaged his neck.

"Sorry boy, I guess I forgot to lock up tonight."

Did he though? The doubt gnawed at his brain like a wolf with a bone, sucking out the marrow of his reason. He heard the door unlock. It was opened. The wind was strong, and the house was old, not entirely impossible that a gust, combined with him maybe not fully closing the door at night, could account for it. But still. The door was made of heavy oak. Not something that would easily be blown open. And Turtle was growling.

As if picking up on his thoughts, Turtle cocked his head to the side and stared into Brian's eyes. His eyes lost the fight against sleep and soon the dog laid down at Brian's feet and dozed off. Brian was also losing that fight. Sitting up on the sofa with the lights on didn't help him win it. Just as he was about to drift off, he turned his head to the side. For just a second, he saw a dark haired woman sitting next to him, curled up into a ball, her face buried in the pillows. Brian's eyes shot open, and his body jolted awake. There was nobody sitting next to him. But Turtle was awake. Sitting on his hind legs in front of that spot, whimpering. Lifting his front paws in the air and pawing at empty space.

Brian drove home from the garage at five p.m. He was a walking nightmare all day. Spilled oil all over the inside of some lady's Mercedes Benz. Even stepped on Bob's foot while he was under the chassis. He didn't sleep at all last night and his head was bobbing down into rest even as he drove his truck through town. Five cups of coffee didn't do shit. Exhaustion. That's what he blamed last night on.

Doors do not just open by themselves. I didn't lock and close it properly. Turtle just got startled by the sudden opening of the door. That's it.

Turtle's pawing at the air? It unnerved him, but just because Cora isn't here anymore doesn't mean he'd just stop doing that, right? Just a reflex.

Brian turned right onto Kavayu Drive. The leafless trees lining the sidewalks clawed up at the ashen sky. A few people were out. Walking their dogs, pushing baby strollers, some wandering with no obvious purpose. He saw a younger couple holding gloved hands as they walked past Tula's Café. The woman was smiling obliviously. All she knew in that moment was joy, was love. The man didn't smile as wide but held a toothless grin. Like an idiot. Brian's eyes tracked them as he passed by. They and the father not too far behind pushing a stroller. And the elderly couple he saw through the cafe's window.

One street is all it took. One section of a small town to show him what he could never have. It was like an entire fucking life from start to end, put on display, all meant to mock him and his loss. He sped up, leaving them all behind. In the rearview mirror, that life and those possibilities shrank to nothingness.

In minutes he was back home. Parked the truck and got out. The sunlight was draining out of the sky. Light touched the top branches of the birch forest surrounding the five homes in the cul-de-sac. Darkness was filling in the paths beneath. Brian walked from the truck to his front door and paused.

A voice. Was that what he heard? It was quiet and soft. It could have been the wind whistling through the trees. He looked at the woods. The woods looked back. He'd been walking those trails for years and never felt watched before as he did in that moment. From the dark and secret places in the forest, he could feel himself being observed and sized up.

He opened the door and went inside. Locked the door. Don't forget the bolt this time.

Turtle was waiting for him. Tail wagging like a windshield wiper.

"Hey guy, miss me?"

Brain took the dog for a walk around the neighborhood. He spent the rest of the evening eating leftover KFC and drinking several cans of Heineken while watching, well he doesn't remember what it was, but he does remember waking up to the evening news report. Some pancake jamboree planned for this weekend out at Tuluoc Park.

He was almost ashamed to find breaded crumbs from his dinner on his chest. He stood and fluffed out his shirt, causing the crumbs to shoot out and scatter. Turtle was on them in nanoseconds. He washed up and shut off the lights. He headed up the stairs to bed.

An hour passed as he stared up at the ceiling in the dark. He wouldn't have been able to say it out loud, but he was afraid to fall asleep. Afraid to wake to another clicking sound from the door. He didn't have to wait until sleep found him though. As he lay wide awake, he heard it.

Click.

Then the sound of metal sliding off metal. The bolt.

A metallic pop as the door unlocked.

Then the explosion of Turtle's barking. He sounded feral, like he was in an actual fight.

Brian flew out of bed, did not trip this time, grabbed his bat and ran downstairs, hitting the lights on as he went.

The front door was wide open.

Turtle was gone.

He heard the barking off in the dark. Brian didn't pause to think. He grabbed a flashlight from the hall closet and ran outside. He had the mind to quickly throw his boots on but was otherwise dressed in only a pair of sweatpants.

He ran out into the front yard and yelled out Turtle's name. A single light from a nearby house turned on. The barking continued from deep in the birch wood forest. Brian ran onto the path. The canopy hid whatever comfort the stars could have brought. Aside from that bouncing beam of light in his hands, everything was pitch black. He ran on autopilot. The barking was pulling away. Off that path he knew so well. Out *there*, into the deep and wild parts of the forest.

The barking stopped. A sharp whimper cut through the night and gouged at his heart. Then all was silent.

"Turtle! Come on, boy, come!"

The trees responded by groaning in the wind.

Brian walked off the path, toward where he thought he heard Turtle's cry. But this was new territory. No paths and no familiar sights to be found here. He slowed his pace to avoid tripping.

He swiped his light left and right and left again. Trees. Bushes. Dirt. Nothing more. He kept on walking, calling out the dog's name. The adrenaline must have been wearing off because he suddenly became aware of how cold he felt. With no shirt on the wind sliced across his skin like thin blades of ice. He shivered and his breathing grew shallow and quick. Everything was collapsing out from under him. He had already lost Cora. He couldn't lose Turtle now. No matter what.

"Brian."

The voice punched out at him from the dark. He twisted around and saw no one. Or did he see a shirt sleeve duck behind a tree just as the light spread over it?

"Hello?" He asked. The sound of his voice spoken aloud in the dark felt out of place.

He moved toward the tree. Walked around it. Nobody there.

A branch snapped. He jerked the light to where he heard it.

"Brian."

The voice came from above. That voice, so soft, so sweet, just like hers.

He pointed the light up. It only revealed bare branches latticed over-head.

Laughter. A woman's. The sound ricocheted off the branches high up.

He couldn't bring himself to say the name that belonged to that voice. Couldn't be possible.

In the distance, something reflected the beam of his flashlight. Like the eyes of an animal at night. Two emerald diamonds glistened.

"Turtle!"

He sprinted towards the eyes.

They darted around a tree before he could get there.

"It's okay buddy, don't be scared. It's me," He said in a high-pitched voice.

Something in Brian's brain froze him on the spot. Some prehistoric animal intelligence hidden away in his amygdala leaked out to the rest of his mind. Some biological wisdom not learned through reason but earned by the survival of his ancestors.

This isn't right.

That's not Turtle.

He would never run from you.

A sudden rush of ice in his veins. Making his skin feel warm by contrast to the cold air.

There were a few animals out here to be wary of. Bears and mountain lions, but that was it. If it was a bear, it was probably already running away. If a cougar—he shifted the light around the forest, especially up in the trees. He heard no rustling. No sounds save for the moans of the trees as the wind picked up its onslaught.

He knew he should back up slowly and make his way out of the forest.

But it could have been a raccoon.

Turtle is still out there.

You stupid asshole, then who's been saying your name?

The fear tugged at his spine to guide him back home. To lead him to the warm living room. The door that—sure not always—but sometimes would lock and keep the bad things away. He could always come back tomorrow.

He recalled the yelp.

He remembered holding that dog as a puppy. Two years ago, he and Cora got him from a family friend. She was beyond ecstatic when he told her she could keep him.

He remembered the three of them huddling together on that sofa as it snowed outside. A wood fire stove burning. Love binding them together.

If he left now, that sofa and that home would be empty forever. That wasn't a life he wanted, no matter what safety was promised in it.

He moved forward. Listening. Moving the light to every conceivable corner an animal could make an approach from.

"Brian."

Unmistakable now. That was Cora's voice. Ahead of him. Behind him. Above him. It was everywhere and nowhere all at once. Was it just in his mind? A cancer of grief rotting away his sanity?

"Turtle!" He shouted.

More laughter. It flowed like the wind through the branches. It threatened to carry him away to seek out its source.

His light landed on a woman's face just as it slipped behind a tree.

His voice stuttered and faltered, "Cora?"

Brian took a step toward the tree. As he neared it, she stepped out in full view of the light. The bright flashlight lit up her face. The tiny nose. The shoulder length black hair. The dimple on only her left cheek. The light was bright, but she didn't even blink.

Brian dropped the flashlight.

The light now only lit up her feet as she turned and ran away.

She was barefoot. In the moment before she turned around, he thought he saw her skin covered in moss.

"Wait! Cora!"

Brian took off after her. She sped away so fast he didn't have time to pick up the light. So scared of losing her trail. He didn't need the light now. Cora's white nightgown gave off a faint pale glow. He couldn't see the ground immediately in front of him, but he could see *her*.

He ran until the cold assaulting his skin was forgotten. Until every muscle was firing so hot he almost felt warm. A branch scratched the skin beneath his armpit. He stumbled and almost fell. Another branch scraped against his forehead. But he kept on running.

Cora's glow was getting smaller, more distant. How fast was she running?

Brian knew, even then in this irrational state, that it couldn't be her. Not alive at least. He remembered the door that opened, unlocked from the inside. He remembered how Turtle pawed at the air last night. Could it be her spirit? He wasn't one to believe in such things, but seeing Cora's face just now settled all doubt. He did not believe he was insane.

Then there was Turtle's yelp of pain and fear. What if it wasn't her?

The glow was a distant firefly of a thing now. Brian pushed his body to run faster.

More branches lacerated his flesh. He could feel the hot and wet stain of blood all over. By some miracle he hadn't fallen over or run right into a tree. Not yet at least. He must have run into a thicker part of the woods where the trees grew closer together. The branch scratches were happening more frequently now. He felt one of them slide across his chest, not from the force of running into it, but because the branch itself moved backwards. Like a claw. Something whipped his back, and he shouted out as he fell to his knees.

Not branches. He saw shadowy things running alongside him. He saw dark and long protrusions, easy enough to mistake for branches in the dark. They were attached to the running things. They giggled in the voices of little girls. A rustle of leaves in front of him. A running shadow slashed his cheek and ran away. Brian covered his face with his hands as a shield. A branch snapped above him. Something grabbed his hair and pulled hard enough to lift him up to his feet. Then it was gone, and he was left with a stinging pain on his scalp. He touched the spot, and his hand felt something wet.

It all stopped. The laughing running things went away or stopped moving to stare at him. The glow reappeared to his left, not more than a dozen or so feet away. Cora looked at him and smiled. He saw a tear run down her cheek, lit up like a crystal refracting the light of her skin's glow. She unfurled her tiny hand and beckoned him with a curled finger.

"Yeah, it's a perfect day," she said. "I'll never get bored."

Then she turned and stooped down to enter a hole. In her glow, Brian could see it was a tunnel made of dead birch trees bent and twisted to form the semicircle that she was now crawling into.

Brian drew near. His heart beat like a jackhammer. This was not possible. But she was there. Right in front of him. And she invited him to join her down that tunnel of sticks and dirt. Giggling and whispering broke out near him.

"Follow her."

"She needs you, Brian."

"She's so alone in death. And you in life. Join her."

"We will feast on your eyes if you linger here, go and be safe with your love."

"Be warm and at home."

"Go, or we will devour your sweet pet."

Cora's face emerged from the tunnel and smiled at him. Just the way she used to when he tried to make her laugh. It even had that slight crookedness on the left side.

Brian knew that face. Whether laughing or crying or even shouting at him, it was that face he had fallen in love with. Maybe this was her. Somehow, she had come back to him. They could be together, forever.

She disappeared back into the tunnel.

"Yes, I will join you," he said.

He bent down and got on his hands and knees. The tunnel was wide enough for him to enter but by no other means. It slanted down and into the earth. Cora's glow dimmed and soon everything was dark as the expanse of space. He could feel something moving down there. He heard the dirt being pushed aside and the wet slide of massive limbs churning over one another. He heard the rumble of a stomach that had not eaten in so very long. He felt the pang in his heart that had not known love even longer.

Barking. From behind him and outside the tunnel. Turtle's bark wrenched his senses back to reality. He could feel his shivering skin. The damp soil soaking his sweatpants. The burning pain of the cuts across his upper torso. The awful damp and rotting moss smell in the tunnel. The realization that this was not Cora. This was something hungry, waiting for him down in the pit. Calling him to it like a siren off the coast.

He backed up, hit his head on the tunnel's roof, lighting up his already sensitive scalp with pain. Something grabbed his right foot. It was Cora. But the glow of her skin had dimmed. The skin was melting away, revealing what looked like a charred skull, sharp teeth with no lips to hide them, and hollowed out eyes. And behind it, something far larger, moving and writhing and twisting down in the deep pit.

He kicked that face that only moments ago had pulled him into that trance of longing, he kicked it as hard as he could with his other foot and the thing let him go.

He pulled himself out of the tunnel and stood and turned in time to see Turtle running up to him in the darkness. The dog whimpered and jumped on Brian's knees. Brian bent down and embraced him. The dog licked his cuts frantically. Brian felt a wet patch on Turtle's shoulders, a cut.

Rage burned away the need to shiver and the need to dive into the pit. There was no reason to join Cora down there. He had reason enough to stay up here and that reason was now growling at the trees.

The running shadows scampered through the branches above. They hissed and made gurgling sounds. Turtle barked and growled and stayed by Brian's side, and he by his. The rumbling from the pit grew like the turning on of some great engine.

There was no way they'd be able to run out of here. Brian had no light, and he doubted that "Cora" would light the way home. The running beings would be on them in moments. Stay and fight seemed the best option.

He balled up his fists, but they shook uncontrollably.

Then, Turtle stopped growling and began whimpering. Not the cry of fear or pain, but the way he used to with Cora. Brian could barely make it out in the dark. He saw Turtle sit on his hind legs and paw up at the air. The rustling in the trees retreated from their position. The rumbling cried out from the pit. The running things didn't make a sound.

"Let's go, boy."

He tugged on Turtle's collar and the dog walked by his side. Brian guessed the way home should have been a straight line from the pit and made his way slowly in the dark, listening for the snap of a branch or the crunch of a leaf. Every so often Turtle whimpered and jumped up at something. But not in aggression. This was out of love and play with something he could not see. He could feel it though, like the air had become warmer.

Brian kept walking despite not being able to feel his fingers anymore. At least the cold numbed the scratches as well. It took them what felt like an hour, but they eventually found the trail. No more hissing from the trees nor the horrid scampering of tiny hooved feet could be heard.

They walked down the trail and came to the cul-de-sac. Brian saw his house, lights still on, front door wide open from when he ran out. They walked inside and he locked the door behind him. He took Turtle into the bathroom and looked in the mirror. His exposed skin striated in dozens of places. Blood had dried in vertical lines from each of the cuts. None of them were deep, but they stung like a bitch. Each group of cuts were three lines etched into his skin, every single one of them. The imprints of small, clawed fingers.

He examined Turtle. The dog had a gash in between his shoulder blades, but nowhere else. Brian got the shower running warm and washed both himself and Turtle off. He dried both of them off and cleaned up Turtle's wound first. The dog winced. He never bared his teeth or ran away. When he had done the best that he could, he walked into the living room and collapsed on the sofa.

Turtle pawed at the space in front of Brian, giving off a small whimper. Out of the left corner of his eye he saw a woman curled up on the couch with him. Turning his head, he saw only cushions there. Only felt the warm air that seemed to envelop him just then.

The Ficus tree caught his attention. He got up and went over to it. The tree had grown a single and vibrant green leaf.

Brian smiled. He didn't need to go out into the woods to find Cora. She was here the whole time.

"Let's go to bed."

Turtle came up with him. He shut the bedroom door. They both got into the bed. Just him and the dog. But that was alright. He could live with it.

PITTER-PATTER GO THE FEET

You wake to a tapping on your window. It started off quiet. So quiet it could have been rain drops falling softly on the glass. You don't believe that, do you?

This isn't the first time you've heard the tapping and the pattering of little feet outside your second story window. Like little people were racing across the side of the house. Each time you've heard it and called for Mom, she came running in to your crying and your blubbering. And each time she told you, "Don't worry dear, it's only wind, nothing to be afraid of."

Her words never worked. Sure, you felt relief while she was in the room, stroking your hair, and hushing away all your fears. But the moment she left, you were all alone. In the dark room, with the window facing the open waters of the lake. Soon the tapping came again. *Tap, tap tap.* A tapping that was trying to get your attention. *Tap, tap tap.* Get you to look over at the window. *Tap, tap tap.* You can't think of an idea more stupid than that. *Tap, tap tap.* You will never look. *Tap, tap tap.*

She won't listen to you. None of the grownups will. They don't believe in magic and monsters and the boogeyman, do they?

Tonight the tapping is the loudest it's ever been. It's growing louder still. You're afraid the glass will crack and something will get in. Something with big ol' teeth and nasty little eyes. Like the giant bird Halloween decorations Mrs. Carruthers keeps on her lawn all year. Mom says she's a loon and you have to agree with her. Who else keeps scary things like that even when it's Christmas?

Insanity.

The tapping is a full on banging now. *Bang, bang, bang.* You're too afraid to peek out from under the covers. *Bang, bang, bang.* Your heart will explode if you should see something at your window. *Bang, bang, bang.* You promised yourself not to look remember? *Bang, bang, bang.* Maybe it will go away if it can't see you? *Bang, bang, bang.* Like the bullies at school. Like Billy the big, red head kid who smells like roast beef. He doesn't bother you much anymore since you've stopped wearing your Pokémon shirts to school.

But no, no dear Ricky, this isn't going to work. The tapping and the pattering and the banging is shaking the wall now. Your Astro Boy picture frame falls off the wall. You hear a sharp *crack* in the glass. You almost pee yourself like you promised Mom and Dad that you'd never do again; like you did at Johnny's house that one time. Big boys don't wet the bed. Big boys don't believe in monsters. Because there is no such thing.

Inspired by your own logic you thrust the covers down off your face. You look. You break the promise with yourself.

Just as Mom opens your door and flips on the lights, you saw something didn't you? In that split second. At the window. You saw the beady red eyes and the long, crooked nose, didn't you? You saw it dip out of view as if it just flew away into the night.

"Mom, there's a monster outside!"

"Ricky," Mom says as she sighs and sits on your bed, hand resting on your blanket-covered knee. "Why were you hitting the window? You woke us up."

"Monsters!"

"Honey, this the third night in a row—"

"Please let me stay with you and Dad tonight! It's gonna get me!"

"I thought you said you wanted to be a big boy? And what do big boys *not* believe in?"

"But I saw it at the window. It flew away when you turned on the lights. It had red eyes like lava."

You jump on the bed and wave your arms around. Maybe the ritual dance will convince her this time?

She furrows her brow and stands up with arms crossed over her chest. "Bed! Now!" You slam down on the mattress in obedience.

She walks over to the window and opens it. How brave she is, you think. Maybe a little stupid too.

"See," she says as she leans out the window and comes back inside. "No monsters hanging on." She shuts the window and locks it. She examines the glass. "Did you throw something at this? There's a big crack."

You shake your head furiously, but she silences you with the hard and freezing stare that only mothers can pull off. She'd give Medusa a run for her money.

"I don't want to hear any more, okay? And tomorrow we'll talk about what chores you can do to pay off this window."

You nod your head, and she seems pleased as she turns off the light and leaves the room. No use in arguing with adults. They never see what you see. They're too busy with things that don't matter like taxes and mortgages and who has the shinier car in the driveway. But you know what matters, don't you? To have a night where you don't shake yourself to exhaustion and then to sleep. To not have to hold in the pee for another night because you're too petrified for your feet to touch the dark floor. Like a black lake. So exposed to the gap under the bed. To not get got by the monsters.

That's what matters, Mom!

No sooner has she left the room than the tapping comes back. *Pitter-patter, pitter-patter.* Not at your window, no, now it's running along the outside wall. The *pitter-patter* of little feet. They run up and down and left and right. *Pitter-patter, pitter-patter.* They stop at the part of your wall nearest your bed. The wall is a few feet away from you, but still, you squirm your body away from it. Just in case. How you wish you could melt into that bed and wake up to the morning. To the smell of pancakes and the opening of presents. You try to imagine that's what Heaven must be like. Those thoughts are wiped away by the tapping. *Tap, bang, tap.* As if each rap against the wall explodes away a single good memory of yours. If it goes on all night, you might not have any left to spare.

At least it's not banging anymore. It's so quiet you're sure that only you can hear it. Maybe Jenna next door, but she told Mom yesterday she heard nothing. What a liar. You saw her face and you know what a stinking liar looks like. She was scared.

You feel better when Mom comes in, but you don't want to make her angry again. Somehow that seems worse than the monster.

Is it even a monster? What did you really see Ricky? It could be a bird. A crow flapping and pecking and tapping against the wall.

Crows don't have red eyes, do they? But you remember that some do. You saw it in a picture book in Mrs. Thompson's class. White-necked crows have those eyes. You should get a star your memory is so good. They're in South America or Antarctica or something, aren't they?

Then you remember.

You regret taking it from Cole, don't you? At first, you didn't think there was a connection. But now, as the footsteps on the wall become louder and louder, *tap, bang, bang.* As your imagination conjures a little man dancing on the wall, you know, don't you? It has to be because of that doll. *BANG, BANG, BANG.*

"Check this out, guys," Cole said as he dumped out his lunch pack over the table. Half an eaten apple and a pack of Dunkaroos spilled out with something else. Something black and hairy. He picked it up and showed it to you and Kenny.

"Whoa!" Kenny gasped.

"Cool, yeah? It's my Grandma's."

"What is it? Looks like a turd monkey," you said.

All three of you laughed at that.

"It's, what did she call it, an eye-doll."

"It's only got two eyes, why's it called that," Kenny asked, making a swipe for the figure as Cole pulled it away.

"Hey, stop it. It's mine. I don't know, that's just what my mom called it. She doesn't like it in the house, but Grandma won't let her get rid of it. Says it's good for keeping bad things away."

"It's creepy," you said. Unable to take your eyes off of those tiny ruby beads it had for eyes. Another part drew your attention. The boots it had on. Like something you saw an Eskimo wearing in a book. They had red ribbons and bells on them. Wouldn't it be cool, you thought, if you could have those? Use them for what? That didn't matter. All that did was that you had them, and Cole didn't.

You waited and you stressed out over it. Until Cole put it back in his backpack and went out to play kickball after school. You returned to the classroom, pretending to read a book inside. Mrs. Thompson called you a good student as you reached for the book about the big red dog. Her words made you feel all warm inside. After, you went to Cole's bag when no one was looking and opened it. Took out the eye-doll. The fur made your hand itch, and you almost dropped it. It was ugly, wasn't it? Droopy hat with a bell on the end, little red eyes, long nose. Face that looked like a dried fruit. You pulled at the boots, and they came off easily. You saw the tiny, clawed feet it had under the shoes and that made you a little sick, didn't it? They looked like a bird's and were so small ten of them could have fit in one boot. You dropped the doll back into the bag and took the boots home.

You didn't tell Cole about it.

Even when he told you yesterday that Grandma was going crazy and running around their house at night. Crying and yelling for the doll. Saying that it needed to be put back.

And now you hear the *pitter-patter* of little feet outside your wall, don't you? *Pitter-patter, pitter-patter.* Silly Ricky, why did you have to steal those boots and leave that ugly thing without something to cover up its ugly feet?

For the first time you think about the boots. They're in your backpack on the floor right now. Maybe if you just give them back, it will stop? But that means getting out of bed in the dark and what if it's under the bed right now? That means opening the window and seeing its tiny little face up close. You're not hero enough for that.

Maybe you won't have to choose. The tapping at the glass has returned. *Tap, tap, tap.* And with it the cracking. Like ice splitting under your shoes when you try to walk out on the frozen shoreline during winter vacation. One time, you even fell in a little and Jenna made fun of you and told on you to Mom. You had to walk all the way back home with soggy socks that made both legs shiver. It's like that now. *Crack.* The glass is about to break, you know it. *Crack.* And something is going to pour into your room and it's going to be worse than cold water. *Crack.*

Your pants are getting warm and wet now. So many promises broken. Get it together, Ricky.

More *rap, rap, tappings,* and *clickity-clacks* dancing across the walls and the glass now. Like there's not just one of them out there. It sounds like they're running all over the house now. *Clickity-clack.* Like the rain got all crazy and dumped everything it had over the roof.

Not rain.

Little footsteps. *Rap, tap, tap.* Sometimes big ones too. *clickity-clack*

The *pitter-pattering* stops.

Another sound breaks in on the moment. You hear Jenna opening her window—you hope it's Jenna. You hear her muffled voice outside.

"Hello?"

At the same time, you hear the window from your parent's room open. Dad shouts something you can't hear clearly.

Whoof kizz dat?

You don't open your window. You know what's waiting for you to do just that.

"Oh my God!" Jenna screams.

You've never really liked her, but all the same you would never wish this on her. You hear her high-pitched scream start from the bedroom, but it's going away. Like it's out by the lake now. Flying away. Carried off by some angry monster bird. You can't hear her anymore.

Dad is shouting louder now, and Mom is screaming too, and everything is loud and scary and you don't know what to do, do you?

You hear somebody running down the hall and Mom's voice is getting louder. Dad says something but gets cut short. All he can make are gargling sounds, like he's at the dentist.

"Ricky! Jenna! Wake up! Run!" Mom screams just outside your door. A light comes on and unfurls under the gap in your door. Then come the *pitter-patter* of little feet in the hall. *Pitter-patter, pitter-patter.* Quickly they come racing down the hall.

You see a big shadow that must be Mom. Then you see the flash of smaller stick shadows moving quickly. They might be legs. Mom screams once more. You hear a heavy *thump* on the floor, and then she goes quiet completely. You hear a sound like someone cutting through something soft. You remember making the same sound last Thanksgiving when you broke the turkey's wishbone and Mom sliced off the meat for you. It's wet at first, but then it *crunches* and *cracks* and there is a *snap*. Two of them. *Snap, snap.* The sounds stop.

Your mattress has joined your pants now. You lie in a warm pool, but you don't mind so much, you're too focused on the sounds, or the lack of them, out in the hallway.

Finally, you do what heroes do. You sit up in bed, you almost call out to Mom but catch the words before they fly out of you. In your heart you know the truth and it makes your lips quiver and your eyes sting. You slip out of bed and land on the floor like a mouse. You're sure you didn't make a sound. But it's so quiet out in the hall that you worry it is listening carefully. Maybe it doesn't know where your room is? Maybe it had to come in through an open window? Maybe it can't open doors?

"Can't eat, maybe?" Mom used to say. The memory is rubbing alcohol on the wound in your heart, and it almost makes you cry out loud. You press your wet hands into your face and smother the sound. You crouch down and find your backpack. Of course, it's under your bed. You get down on your hands and knees and reach for it. You grab it and pull it out.

You think the boots are in the small pouch where you keep your colored pencils. You grab the zipper and slowly, so slowly, begin to unzip the bag. *Ziiiip.* The sound is like a knife cutting across the silence. You hold your breath like that was the problem. No sounds from the hall. But there is movement across the light under the gap in the door. The shadowy sticks move to each end of the door. The lower parts of the sticks look fatter now.

You unzipped the bag just big enough to slip your hand inside. The teeth of the opened zipper scrape against the back of your hand. You feel the small notebooks and the pencils and maybe the squish of a forgotten banana you were supposed to eat at school but forgot like always. Then you feel the furry boots. You grab them and pull them out of the bag.

The tapping is rapping against your bedroom door now. Like someone is knocking but they won't stop and be polite about it.

Tap, tap, tap, tap, tap.

The shadow sticks in the gap are dancing around now like the knocker is growing impatient.

Tap, tap, tap, tap, tap.

You hold the boots tight in your palm and half walk, half crouch your way towards the door. *Tap, tap, tap, tap, tap.*

Maybe you shouldn't open it. Maybe it can't really get in. But then what? Live in the room for the rest of your life? *Tap, tap, tap, tap, tap.*

As you walk across the dark room, you notice something by the window.

A little flash of red.

You turn your head and then wish you hadn't.

You see the red beady eyes at the window. Much larger than the doll's. You see the smile full of silver teeth. The droopy hat, much too big, even for Dad, with the bell glinting some porch light outside. It doesn't move out of the way or try to hide from you. It raises a fist and taps against the glass.

Tap, tap, tap, crack.

You see the glass fall into the room. The smiling thing looks down and then back up at you. It shakes its head and the bell tinkles like you think Santa's reindeer do when they come in through your chimney at night. *Jingle, jingle.*

Then you hear the *creak* of your bedroom door behind you as it opens. The tapping stops.

The thing at the window is gone. The pattering of feet behind you is growing loud and heavy. *Pitter-patter, pitter-patter.* The tinkling of a bell with every step. *Jingle, jingle.*

The light from the hall fills your room and you see your own shadow stretch from your feet to the broken window. Then you see a bigger shadow that swallows your own. You close your eyes and hold out the boots.

"P-p-please." That's about all you can say. You hold out the boots hoping it will take them and go.

"No, t'ank you. I won' be needing dems no more. And yours ain't right is dey?"

The voice is that of a child's. Younger than you. Maybe a girl, maybe a boy. The accent is funny, you almost don't understand what it says. You hear the *pitter-patter* of heavy feet scuttle out of your room and then in the hall and then down the stairs. You hear the front door open but don't hear it close.

You stay like that, eyes closed, legs shaking so hard your knees clack together. *Clack, clack.* You almost fall to the ground and have a good cry.

No, that's not what heroes do. You open your eyes and turn around. You see Mom lying there in the hall. You walk over to her. You see her eyes opened and not blinking and her mouth shaped like a scream. You look down at her legs and notice red streaks are across the lower part of her blue pajama pants. The same pants you and Jenna picked out for her last year for her birthday. The ones with the little bears throwing snowballs stitched across them. You look further down and see the bloody pink bunny slippers not on her feet.

Because she has no feet.

THE THING IN THE CLOSET

"**A**ll I have is you. Precious Thing. You keep me going. When life knocks me down, by golly, I get right back up, don't I?"

I let out a wheezing laugh that quickly turns into a coughing fit. I keel over to my knees and hammer my fist into my sternum to clear my throat. Once I've done that whole mess I look back at the Thing in the closet. There on my knees, I feel the sudden urge to press my face onto the floor. So I do. This is sacred ground, and I must kiss the sanctuary whereupon It's feet alight. I kiss the floor. Saliva mixes with the dust and clods of other filth fly up into my throat when I inhale. The coughing resumes and I have to squirm on the floor like the worm that I am just to breathe. I thrash about like an epileptic until the coughing subsides.

I pick up my feeble body, using the bedside to support me. It feels like my spine may very well snap in two at any moment now. My bulbous head is far too heavy for my thin neck. I'm too ashamed to look back into the closet. I've embarrassed myself before It. Stupid. Stupid. Stupid.

I smack my face with each utterance of that word in my mind. It ought to become my new moniker.

"That would be appropriate and well-mannered, it sure would."

I approach the closet and give the Thing one last look. A tear rises into my left eye and spills out over my cheek. It will be so lonely while I am away. I close the doors. Latch the hook lock. Can't let that sordid business happen again, forgetting the locks. There are only so many times I can move house on such a meager paycheck.

My bare feet walk across the grimy floor of the bedroom to the grimy floor of the bathroom. My feet stick to the tiles as I go. I take off my clothes and let them fall where they may. I turn on the water for the shower and at first the pipes make a groaning sound before spewing out the rust-colored liquid. I enter the curtain of ice-cold water and embrace it. This is my cleansing. This is my ritual of ablution before entering the real filth of the world, the society of others. And today is an important day, by Jove!

I finish washing myself the best I can and dry off with my towel, which is now nothing more than a tattered and moldy cloth. I suppose it does smell something rank, but I can't notice it anymore. I put on my white dress shirt, khaki slacks, and brown shiny shoes. They don't fit so well anymore. Especially the shoes, they bend my toes and snap off the nails. These may be the only items left in the apartment not touched by the encroaching slime of entropy. I make sure they stand apart. Not because I care, but because they, other people, will not accept me any other way. These clothes are vital to me. They are my mask. My shield and my passport as I go out and mix among the heathens. But the grime of my flesh sticks to them anyway.

I take a comb that was lying on the floor under the bathroom sink and swipe away the few graying strands of hair across my otherwise bald head. I smile at the murky mirror. I can almost see my teeth. I'd rather not describe them, thank you very much. Let's just say I probably shouldn't smile often while I am out and about. Unless I'm in trouble, of course.

"What a wonderful day it will be, indeed." I wink at the mirror the color of raw milky sewage and gesture my hand like a gun. That's the ticket. Charisma and charm, dear Maxwell. Charisma and charm.

I walk through my living room. The lights flicker and buzz and give off a pale green radiance that makes me feel like I'm underwater. Dead flies line the bottom casing of the light fixtures. It's too dark to see my walls, but I think they were blue at one time. Or maybe red? Who can keep track of such things?

I laugh out loud, and the shrill spike of my voice immediately fills me with shame.

Stupid. Stupid. Stupid.

Slap. Slap. Slap.

My cheeks must be red now because they feel warm. That will surely help me when I hit the January morning streets and give the world my best!

I make for the front door and unlock the three deadbolts. Each of them screeches against the rusty metal and makes my nerve endings, I mean my teeth, hurt.

Fear grips me. I don't know why. I run back to the closet and unlock the latch. I throw open the doors and fall to my knees.

The Thing in the closet is still there. I smile and I feel glad.

"Give unto me an ounce of the grace of this holy of holies and I can accomplish the task at hand. I beg you."

The Thing doesn't respond to me. Is it cross with me? I weep and I throw my face down to the floor and kiss it again. I must have hit the ground too hard because my nose stings and I see blood dripping down and coloring the floor in tiny little drops of red. The clothes on the hangers shift and make a rattling sound. The Thing is suddenly aware and keenly interested in my presence. I quickly stand to my feet and shut the doors. I hear It licking the floor.

I wash the blood off my face in the kitchen sink. The water there is blacker than the shower's. I don't bother drying my face, the cold air will do me so good, gosh darn it.

I leave my apartment and lock the door behind me. Can't forget the locks, dear Maxwell.

I take a deep breath. "You can do this my boy."

Before I leave Mrs. Cormac shouts at me from down the hall. "Max! Keep it down in there. I don't know what the fuck you do all night and who the fuck you got tussling 'round in there. Keep it up and I'm callin' the cops."

She slams her door shut.

She mustn't call the cops, no sir, not yet. After tonight? Who cares?

Oh Blessed Thing, do behave Yourself.

"Max! Got a mess in the men's stalls. Some asshole pissed all over the walls by the urinals."

The words wake me out of my trance. I was staring at the linoleum lined hallway. The shine and the sheen make me sick.

"Max, did you hear me? Fucking weirdo," Carlos barks at me.

"Y-yes sir. I'm on it, you c-c-can always count on me. Or, or my name's not Maxwell Gladstone." I smile and Carlos winces at the sight.

"Whatever, man, just get out of here and do your job. Better yet, how about I just don't see you for the rest of the night. Go busy yourself in the stalls and stay there, will ya?"

I salute and click my heels. I grab my mop and bucket and cart them off toward the men's restroom. I hear Carlos mutter "retard" before I've even left the office. That's not very nice of him, is it? No dignity to hold one's tongue until said object of conversation is out of earshot.

I walk down the hallway and when I'm confident I'm alone I say, "No, no, this won't do."

Red colors my vision. My heart beats in my throat. I see myself taking the mop handle and shoving it straight through Carlos' eye. Sticking him to his shiny floor. Like Vlad the Impaler used to do to all those nasty naysayers.

"No, no, no. There is a time and a place for all things. One day the whole wide world will be washed anew in Its grace. Keep the course, my dear Maxwell, keep the course and all shall be revealed."

I open two heavy metal doors that swing inward. The lights make my eyes hurt in here. The electric pings of the slot machines and the heavy smoke clouds and the jibbering and the jabbering of all the heathens makes me want to do it now! Yes, do it now and show them!

Calm down, Maxwell. Soon enough. When the Thing has command-ed it.

"Hey, babe, check this guy out," says the man with the cheap knock-off cowboy hat by the craps table. He's wearing mirrored sunglasses and has an oversized cigar hanging out of his mouth. A woman, a good twenty years younger than him, spins around in her seat so fast her skirt twirls up like Marilyn Monroe's and I see her pink panties. Heat fills my groin and shame fills my head. I want to slap my face but I can't. Not here. Not yet.

She laughs at me in her falsetto voice like a seagull as I pass them by.

"Oh...my...God. Do you smell that?" says the woman.

"Like a walkin' dumpster fire full o' shit," says the man.

I flash them a "How do you do, neighbor?" smile and wink at them.

"Cheery d-d-day to the lot of you, dear sir and m-m-madam," I say in my best Sunday voice. I pretend to tip my non-existent hat and grin my toothless, but not empty, grin.

Oh, I shouldn't have done that.

They aren't laughing anymore. I don't stay to see what happened. I've seen it enough, haven't I? I do hear the crowd cry out in surprise as a table flips over and somebody crashes to the floor. I hear the cowboy hat man yell out in terror.

I hope the security cameras didn't catch any of that nastiness. But what does it matter? Just one more day and I can be with the Thing forever in a blissful paradise. It has promised me UNION. I just need to hold on for another few hours is all. Just have to make it to the end of today without drawing too much attention to myself. If someone were to find the Thing before the time, oh, perish the thought.

I start to silently weep as I make way across the casino floor, dodging stumbling customers too blitzed out of their minds by alcohol and greed to notice me. I finally reach the men's restroom and walk in.

True to Carlos' word, somebody has pissed all over the urinals. And the walls. And the floor as well. The ammonia scent fills my nostrils and I sigh in ecstasy. I can even taste it on my tongue. Like the finish of a fine wine.

I almost don't want to waste it all on the mop. But a job is a job and if my bitch mother never told any true thing in her life she at least told me that.

"And that's a f-fact, Jack," I say to myself in the mirror. My mouth hangs slack-jawed and a dribble of drool hangs out. I look so stupid. Oh, I know it. Don't take me for a fool, I could not bear that! This is the way it has to be though. One must go before all others to prepare the way for the Thing.

These mirrors are clear, well, mostly clear. I miss the murkiness of my own bathroom mirror. I see too much of my own face in these ones. The wrinkled forehead, the wispy hair, the moles dotting my cheeks, the black maw of a mouth where my white teeth once stood proudly on display. All my teeth are black. Okay, I've told you now are you happy? They are lumps of rotting coal and oh, how they hurt at all times. Even breathing is too much for my nerve endings. Any heat and any cold that touches the tips sends my whole skull into electric shock.

Who needs them anymore when I have the Thing? They were a small price to pay for true wisdom. I mop up the urine and it makes a *swish* sound. I imagine gargling it and spitting it back out onto Carlos' fat face. I laugh shrilly and it echoes off the tiled walls.

Job all done. Right as rain and all that. The floors are disgustingly clean now. I resisted the temptation to get on my hands and knees and take of the blessed communion this time. After today, there will be eons before me to partake.

The doors swing open. It's the cowboy hat man. Blood is streaming down his forehead. He's being carried by two men, maybe his friends, they have him in between them. They lead him to the sink right next to me and splash water on his face. He still won't take those stupid sunglasses off. He presses a cloth to his head and finally looks up and sees me.

"The fuck did you do to me?" He says as he pushes the two men away from him. He rolls up his sleeves like a Saturday morning cartoon, the kind I used to watch with Uncle Jimmy until I wasn't allowed to be with him no more.

"I d-didn't do n-n-nothing, kind sir," I say and hold out the mop between us as if it will protect me.

I could do it again. I could ask the Thing to come and aid me again. To show Itself in my smile. But back at the craps table was selfish of me. If I push my luck, the Thing might not hear me when it really counts. Others might notice and take It away from me!

I close my eyes and let the fists come smashing into my face.

I dream in fragments and pieces. I dream of a blonde-haired man with straight teeth. He has a wife and a son. His clothes do not smell like rot and his skin does not smell of stale sweat and disease.

I wake and feel lonely. Like I have lost something.

Silly Maxwell, what have you lost when all has been found!

I know it has been ten minutes that I have been dreaming by my wristwatch, I wake in a daze on the freshly cleaned bathroom floor. My head hurts and I taste blood in my mouth. The bathroom is not as clean as I remember it being. That pungent aroma of piss, that warm and delectable moistness, it's all over me now. I wake up fully and realize that man must have peed on me. My shirt and my face are wet.

I get on my knees and raise my hands to the ceiling.

"Ablution of the saints. Holy Communion."

I squeeze my shirt to get precious drops of it into my mouth like a man dying of dehydration. The sweetness of it runs down my mouth.

Then the door opens and Carlos walks in.

"Holy shit! I knew you was a freak. Get the fuck up."

I rise to my feet like the newly resurrected ones. Like the ones that are to come.

"Max, I'm tired of all this shit. You creep out the customers. And I walk in on you like this? You're fired. Grab your shit and get the fuck outta my face."

He leaves and lets the door shut behind him. I look at my wristwatch. I didn't make it to the end of my shift. Only had one more hour to go.

Panic seizes me. I whine like a child. I tear at my wispy hair and pull out a few of the remaining strands. Now there is almost nothing left.

"I'll be caught in the cold and without a cap upon my head."

The Thing will be most displeased with me. And on the cusp of what was to be our blessed union!

Why? Why did the Thing want me to stay at work all day? It has never commanded me as thus before. Think, Maxwell, think!

Could it be? Will It leave me tonight? Has It taken another disciple unto Itself?

"Well, that's all fine and dandy, leave a gentleman without a partner in the dance."

Rage boils in my guts. I must get home, now!

But first, I should call upon Carlos one last time.

I've used all my strength to bring him here. My mouth is dry like cotton balls. My joints make a grinding sound as I walk.

Carlos is in a daze, walking beside me up the steps to my apartment. Blood is trailing from his eyes, and he doesn't know where he is or what it is he is doing, does he?

My shrill laugh destroys the stillness of the stairwell.

I don't feel ashamed this time. That's new.

All I had to do was smile at him and he immediately caved in to me. That is the power of the holy of holies, my friend!

I push Carlos up the stairs whenever he dithers and dathers. Eventually, we make it to my door.

The Thing will be so pleased with me. I brought It a succulent feast to last it for a week! No more rats and cockroaches, my friends!

Carlos stops at my door, and I push past him to open it.

"No, no, no, no!" I scream and stand there in fright. My door is wide open.

Like a flash flood the memory comes back to me. My failure. The one thing I should have been most careful to observe. I forgot to latch the closet door!

I notice the black ash trail coming out of my apartment. It goes down the hall to Mrs. Cormack's room. The one who always beats against the wall between us to tell me to be quiet while I dance in reverie before the Thing.

Carlos flutters his eyes. His throat makes a grunting noise. He is waking up. I go into my apartment and grab the heavy iron bar I keep in the corner. I come out to the dimly lit hall and strike the side of Carlos' head.

I don't think he is dead. The foot is dancing, see! There is a lot of blood on the ground though.

"G-g-guess I'll have to mop it up!"

I want to laugh until I remember the task at hand. I also realize that I must clean up quickly before anyone else notices what is happening. I drop the bar and run to Mrs. Cormack's room. The door is opened halfway. The ash trail goes right through the little gap. She must have opened the door for the Thing.

"Very p-polite indeed, Mrs. Cormack."

I push the door open and it squeals like I do while lying naked on my face before the open closet door.

The lights are off, and it is very dark indeed.

"O' Blessed One, take not what you do not need. I have brought you enough. Out in the hall. Come and sup!"

I walk into the apartment and turn a corner. I see the flickering light of the TV and the silhouette of a recliner. I see the slippers on the feet of an elderly woman, hanging off the side of the chair like she is sitting in it sideways. On the other side of the chair her hair in curlers shows itself. The chair rocks and her body falls to the floor. The feet go one way. The head goes another and rolls off under the coffee table. A dark shape runs across the floor and straight into my open arms.

"O dear child, dear Thing. O Blessed One, let me take you home."

I grab a throw blanket off Mrs. Cormack's sofa.

"She won't be n-needing this now, will she, dear?"

I laugh and cover the Thing with the blanket. It shivers and quakes in my arms.

I walk back out into the hall and into my own apartment.

Wait a darn second. Carlos wasn't there.

Before I can act on this, before I can return the Thing to Its throne, I see him.

Bloodied face. Sweat glistening off his forehead. The stench of when he let go of his bowels while we walked up the stairs. O Carlos, you thing of beauty.

He's holding the iron pipe.

"You sick fuck! Did you drug me?"

He sways and he swoons a bit.

"What do you have in your hands? Fucking drop it."

"N-n-no, dear sir. I mustn't let the Prince free before It's time. Heathens cannot handle the glory of what It has to show."

He is not listening to me. Poor stupid man. If you would have just let me take you into the closet before you woke, there would be no you to worry about things like this. But now...you leave me no choice.

Carlos lunges at me with the pipe held high.

I drop the Thing onto the floor and the blanket falls off It.

Carlos freezes in place and drops the pipe. His hands shake so hard. I'm not surprised. I see his jeans grow dark where he wets himself. He falls on his knees and the sweat comes off his face like a fountain!

The Thing starts small. It looks like an ape in a way. But the spine and the legs are too short and the arms are too long. And It grows. Oh, how It grows.

The black matted fur writhes like living snakes. Its spine extends and now Its head touches the ceiling. Its arms touch opposite walls of the room at the same time. I can't see Carlos anymore and I can't even hear the man scream. All I hear is a murmuring and a pathetic attempt to speak. A stink that even I can sense fills the room. It makes me gag and I partake of the Communion of Its odor.

The Thing shrinks back down to Its child size and runs off to my bedroom. I notice that Carlos is still on his knees as I run after It and see the closet door shut. I lunge at the door and hook the latch with the runes carved on it. I go back to the living room, now covered from wall to ceiling in the black film of Its presence. Carlos is still alive. He is weeping. His shirt is drenched in sweat.

I get down on my knees before him and grab his hands. "O, dear brother, It has chosen you to serve alongside me!"

I laugh. I cry. Carlos embraces me and our sweat intermingles. We are brethren of the Thing now.

Carlos speaks, "I d-d-d-on't know what is happening, but, gosh darn it, I feel chipper."

"Top dollar bill comment, dear chap," I say. I help him to his feet and lead him to the closet. The doors rattle.

"W-w-what is It?" Carlos says.

"Would you like to come and see? We can sup at Its table, you and I. And soon, all the others will join us. And tonight is the Night of UNION."

He nods like a child who has lost his parents. I take his hand and lead him to the Temple.

We kneel before the locked door. The door shakes and the lock rattles. The black tendrils of Its presence wiggle through the cracks in the rotten wood.

"What is going to happen?" Carlos asks.

I do not answer him. For I do not know what it shall look like. I flip the lock open.

The doors open.

And tide of Its presence washes over us.

UBUME

Another scream.

More crying.

Wailing the likes of which Megumi had never heard before. She sat up in bed, covered in a sweat that made her shiver. Rain pelted her window and the aluminum roof. Metallic pings rang throughout the box that was her one room apartment and banged their way into her skull.

The screaming ended.

Megumi stayed awake, wondering if she had actually heard those sounds coming from outside or not. In the dark room she made out the rough forms of her dresser by the wall, of the pile of dirty clothes by the foot of her bed, of the litter box in the corner by the front door. Her cat, Latte was nowhere to be found, he was probably fast asleep in the pile of clothes, oblivious to the horrible noises.

The screams started again.

They were coming from right outside the window behind her bed. The high-pitched and tortured shriek was a woman's.

Megumi pulled the covers off and got out of bed. Her feet touched the cold floor and a pin prick sensation shot through her soles. It made her teeth hurt. Latte meowed from behind her on the bed. Apparently, there the whole time.

She went over to the window and pushed the curtain out of the way. A single streetlight burned white in the darkness. The rain fell in heavy torrents. Blanketing the world in obscurity. The screaming was coming from the river that ran adjacent to the five-story apartment complex that she lived in. The rain beat loudly against the building. So loud that Megumi questioned why she was able to hear the screams in the first place.

She squinted into the darkness. As if responding to her attempt to see more, a figure came into view below the streetlight. Megumi could see white and red coloring of the clothing, which looked vaguely like a robe. She was holding a bundle in front of her, rocking back and forth, walking in fidgeting movements.

That's just the rain making it look that way.

The figure screamed again and fell to her knees. She lifted the bundle up and struck it against the ground.

Megumi was glued to the window. She wished somebody would run out there and help the woman. It wasn't going to be her, that was for sure.

She overcame her inaction and reached for her phone on the bedside table. Dialed the police and told them about the woman. They assured her that somebody would be sent out soon to check. She hung up and kept looking out the window. Latte jumped up on the sill and nuzzled her elbow with his nose. She absentmindedly scratched his head as he purred.

The woman rose to her feet, holding the bundle to her side with one hand like a child with a toy, letting it almost drag on the ground. She lifted her head and seemed to be staring up at Megumi's apartment. The rain was too intense to tell for sure. The woman's face was hidden behind the blurring effect of the rain. She didn't scream again. Just stood there listlessly, barely holding onto the bundle. Her head cocked to one side and rested there. Long black hair draped down to her waist. She swayed and Megumi feared she might faint.

Megumi didn't know how long she stayed there looking at the woman in the dark. She had kept the lights off. What she did become aware of, when the flashing lights of the patrol car came into the parking lot, was that Latte was already asleep again on the bed.

She watched as the car came into view and parked. She moved her gaze back to the streetlight, but the woman was gone. A cop stepped out of the car dressed in a black raincoat. His partner joined him, shining their flashlights around as they made their way to the streetlight Megumi told them about. They walked past the light and toward the riverbanks beyond. She lost sight of them and their lights for a few moments.

The downpour lessened to a drizzle. She could make out the shadowy lines of the river, like a black gash cut out of the night. Two lights shined out by the water. They came closer until the streetlight revealed the officers again. They spoke to each other and got back into their car. After a minute or two the car pulled away and they were gone.

The rain came to an end. A few stars poked out from behind the storm clouds.

Did they find her? Is she okay?

She knew they most likely did not find the woman. They came back far too quickly to have actually done anything of use. Megumi shut her curtains and went back to bed. Latte refused to budge and give her space to lay down straight. She curled up into a ball at the head of the bed. Before she fell completely asleep, she thought she heard the cry one last time. A faint whistle of wind on the night. Then darkness took her.

"I'm...so happy for you," Megumi said forcing a smile.

"It's great, isn't it!?" Reina exclaimed and clasped her hands together like she was praying. "I hope it's a boy. I've always wanted a boy. I mean, a girl would be nice too, don't get me wrong, but a boy would just be, you know, a different experience, right? What do you think I should name him? I was thinking Kaito or Ryu. Are you planning on having kids anytime soon?"

Megumi tried to tune out the insect buzz of Reina's overenthusiasm but was losing that fight. "Someday, maybe."

The chime for the front entrance rang. Reina spun on her heels and ran over to the front of the store. "Welcome! Can I help you find anything today?"

Megumi let out a long sigh. Some relief at last. She moved to the back of the store and busied herself with opening up a box of new inventory and hanging the shirts on the valet rod. Reina's voice filled the store, even all the way to the back. Megumi smiled as she noticed she didn't give the customer a moment to respond. It might not have been the most humane tactic, but Reina did hold the record for the most sales at the store. Holding people hostage with cheerfulness was a skill Megumi didn't care to learn.

The smile didn't last long. Reina's words about having a baby cut open old wounds. She knew it wasn't her fault; she didn't know the details of Megumi's life. But still, she hated that bitch then.

She picked out an olive-green dress from the box and took it out of the plastic wrapping. She stuck on the store's price sticker and hung it. The color reminded her of the hospital gown she wore two years ago. Combined with Reina's sickly exuberant announcement, Megumi found herself back in a nightmare.

"Tachycardia, sustained heart rate above 160 bmp."

The beep of the monitor, what was a soothing rhythm of reassurance a minute ago, was now a frantic warning bell.

Her own heart was trying to escape her chest, and blood was pouring between her legs and over the delivery table. The stark contrast of wet scarlet and clinical white is something she can still see today. Every time she closes her eyes, in fact.

Pain erupted from deep in her bowels. She felt like the baby was splitting her apart.

Memories became fuzzy at this point. She could recall people running in and out of the room. Medical jargon that was beyond her understanding being shouted out. The nerve scorching pain. And the beeping. It rose above the rest of the chaos.

Like an urgent call of distress, the beeping came in rapid fire succession.

Then it flatlined. One tone that didn't change its pitch.

Then darkness.

She was alone in that void. She could only hear. *Beeeeeeeeeeeeeep.*

Taichi didn't stick around long after that. It wasn't that they hated each other, but that they reminded each other of what they had lost. Every glance a slap in the face. Every word spoken a tearing of the bandages.

And Reina brought that all back today.

Megumi's chest cavity felt empty. As if all her insides had been scooped out and replaced with heavy ice.

She pushed the green dress down the rod and reached for another from the box. Reina came prancing back from the front of the store.

"Hey, you're looking glum. What's wrong? You know what really helps me when I'm down? Yoga on a grassy lawn!" She nearly squealed these words out. "But I don't think that would be good for the baby, I don't know, what do you think?"

Megumi sucked in a lung full of air in preparation to answer. But this was Reina. There would be no need. She started talking about how she was going to go and get her poodle's hair done later that afternoon. She walked away to take care of another customer, chattering away. It didn't matter if Megumi was there or not, all she needed was a listening ear. And Megumi was glad for it.

She finished unpacking the box and took her lunch break. Headed out to the riverbanks with a tuna rice ball she bought on the way at a convenience store. A few hundred people were out walking the narrow alleyways and strolling along the river that ran parallel to the city's main shopping area. Couples and families, foreign tourists, and the more eccentric types. There was even a man who would walk his pet meerkat on occasion.

She walked down a set of stone steps that led from the shopping arcade and down to the river. She found a spot on a stone bench under the Sanjo Bridge. Some privacy away from the crowds. The river was a leap away from the bench. It was as wide as a four-lane highway and the water ran quickly due to the heavy rains they've been getting.

The sky was sapphire blue. A slight chill carried with the wind. Golden sunlight washed over everything on the crisp autumn afternoon. The temperature wasn't especially low, but there was no escape from the ever-present cold air. One of Kyoto's finest traits, being situated in a basin. There was no escape from the heat in summer or the cold in winter. Just as she had no escape from nightmares of losing her daughter two years ago. Nor of the more present worry-- the woman in the rain.

She hadn't left Megumi's mind since last night.

What was she doing there? Alone in the storm. And what was she carrying?

She took a bite out of her rice ball and then lit a cigarette. The city recently made smoking outside of designated areas illegal. She was sure the few people walking by her wouldn't mind. She had seen a group of tourists, Spanish she thought, smoking as they walked down the road and nobody said anything, not even the police.

Useless. I bet they saw her last night and decided they didn't want to deal with a mentally disturbed homeless woman.

Megumi wasn't one to pry into the business of others. But she couldn't shake off the image of the rain drenched woman. Screaming and striking the ground. She needed help last night and nobody gave it to her.

Megumi smoked the cigarette down to the butt, threw it on the ground, and stamped it out.

She got up and started to ascend the steps. She stopped and turned around, looking out at the river. The riverbanks stretched on for miles, but Megumi's place was nearby. The chances of that woman being here today was high. Megumi scanned the people and quickly stopped. She didn't know what the woman looked like. So, what was she looking for?

Fidgeting and rickety steps? Fists striking the ground? Impossibly loud wailing?

She decided then and there to help that woman. Tonight. If she ever saw her again.

Megumi entered her apartment and locked the metal door behind her. Her arms were busy carrying two bags of groceries and Latte was busy attacking her shins with his claws. She scolded him but smiled. She set the bags down on a circular table, put the perishables away, poured the cat his dry food, even mixed in some meat she picked up special for him. She didn't know what kind of meat, but it did say PREMIUM on the can so it must be good.

The sun was a thin strip of red on the horizon and the light filled her room in a vibrant haze. She walked over to the window and looked out at the river. It ran like blood. She shut her eyes to the unwanted image of the delivery table that came barging into her mind. A rumble of thunder over the mountains that shadowed the city interrupted those thoughts. Dark clouds were spilling over the peaks and heading for her neighborhood. She saw the curtain of rain falling in the distance. They were moving quickly. The storm would hit in minutes.

She turned on the electric kettle and sat down on her pink beanbag chair by the window, waiting for the water to boil. The sun dipped fully beneath the mountains, creating clear gray splashes across the sky. It soon turned black as the storm clouds crossed the river and enveloped the apartment complex in a light rain.

The kettle chimed. Megumi went over and prepped a cup of tea. Latte, a fat and old cat, had already run out of energy and lay in a coma in the middle of the room. Megumi distracted herself from thinking of the woman as she cleaned up the dirty pile of laundry and watched a singing contest on TV. Hours passed. She shut off all the lights and went to bed. The ping of the drops against the roof were a soothing tapping rather than the clanging assault of the previous torrent.

Maybe that's why she heard it this time. Not the screaming. She heard a woman's voice, speaking calmly, outside her window. Megumi hadn't fallen asleep yet. She lay in bed wide eyed. Though she couldn't hear the words, the voice was loud. Too loud to be heard so clearly from outside.

At first, she thought she may be imagining the voice. Until the speaking became screaming. She sat up and went to the window to peer out.

There she was again. Under the streetlight. The rain wasn't as thick as the other night and now Megumi could clearly see that the woman was cradling a bundle to her chest still. It was wrapped in a dirty white cloth. The woman was also wearing a white robe. Or what was at one time white. She could see the red stains from her waist down to her ankles. It was bright and shone in the dark. She twitched her head to the side, her whole body shaking, her voice wailing.

Megumi called the police again. They again said they would come out and look. She hung up, but didn't wait for them this time. She grabbed a flashlight from a box above her kitchen sink, threw on a raincoat over her pajamas, and slipped into her Crocs. She left her apartment and made her way outside to the parking lot. The rain let up some and became not much more than a mist. She could see the streetlight from under an alcove of the apartment complex, directly in front of her, across the parking lot. The woman was there, she showed no signs of responding to Megumi's presence. The woman turned sharply to her left and stumbled into the darkness beyond the light.

For a moment Megumi hesitated. She could just wait for the cops to come. But what if the woman walked further away and they couldn't find her again?

Megumi jogged across the lot and stood in the center of the streetlight's halo. She could see a shadow walking further away and down to the river.

"Hey! Wait! I can help you!" Megumi shouted and then took off after the woman. She was facing the water with her back to Megumi. Swaying side to side. Arms out of sight, in front of her own chest, clutching the bundle. Her crying died down to a pathetic whimper. Like a dog might do while begging for food.

"Miss? Are you hurt?"

Megumi walked closer. She didn't want to shine her flashlight on the woman and blind her so she kept it focused on the ground in front of her. The mist came in sideways, bypassing her hood and blowing directly into her face. She squinted against the rain and the woman was now facing Megumi.

I didn't see her move. Could be the rain's fault.

Megumi took one more step towards the woman and stopped. The smell of rotten meat filled her nose and mouth. She gagged. Was it coming from the woman?

She shined the light at the woman's feet. She was barefoot. They were bright red and dark purple and bloated. The woman's robe glistened with what Megumi could now tell was blood. It was tattered and shredded. The blood rose to the lower half of her chest, the rest of the robe was white and clean, almost as if the woman had been dipped in blood by her head. In the gaps of the robe, Megumi could see her skin; purple, green, red, bloated like the feet, an exposed rib, and decomposing flesh on her forearms. The bundled and bloody object in her arms was in the shape of an infant.

And her face...Megumi stopped breathing. The woman was missing her lower jaw. The tongue hung loose and flapped around like a necktie on a windy day. The eyes were milky white with no discernible iris. The woman stopped whimpering. Her head jerked to the river and then back to Megumi like the head of an insect. The woman—the thing—lifted the bundle up and seemed to offer it to Megumi.

Megumi took a step back, almost tripping over a tuft of grass.

The woman-thing herself recoiled at Megumi's retreat. She screamed; a cry that froze Megumi's blood and brought her crashing to her ass. The woman lifted the bundle up and smashed it into the ground. Megumi heard a crunch and a snap.

Then the woman was gone. Nothing there, but light clouds of mist and the black and raging river beyond it.

She picked herself up and fled back into the apartment. She flew up the stairs, not even waiting for the elevator. Ripped open her door and locked it behind her. Latte jumped up in the air off her bed and scurried away behind the curtain. She tore off her raincoat and Crocs and dropped the flashlight on the floor.

She turned off the lights and dove under her covers. She scrolled through her phone for somebody to call. The police were already on their way.

But what could she say to them?

Please help, I saw a ghost?

No, they wouldn't believe her. She knew what she saw wasn't a person, not a thing that an officer could do anything about. She resolved to wait until she saw the patrol lights down in the lot and go to speak to them. Maybe if they were there in person, it might make her case more believable.

She waited in the dark for the flashing lights. Checking her phone, she saw that almost thirty minutes passed with her welded to her blankets. At least Latte came out of hiding and jumped up onto the bed and curled up by her feet, falling asleep immediately. She began to laugh to herself. Maybe she hadn't actually seen what she thought she did? She almost convinced herself of that.

That was until Latte raised his head. His ears stood straight up, and he glimmered with an alertness she hadn't seen him possess since he was a kitten. She could see his muscles tense even under all that fur and fat. There was an invisible electric charge. He arched his back and hissed at the window behind Megumi's head.

There was no fire escape or any other structure outside that window. Nothing but empty space standing three stories above the parking lot. The fear took hold regardless. She imagined someone—*her*—hovering in the air, peering through the curtain and down at her. The streetlight cast a sickly light into the room, painting a white stripe from the left side of her bed down to the front door. This was something that had always annoyed her, but now she found some comfort in it. Until she saw the shadow rise. The black thing stretched all the way to the door. Wispy tendrils of hair whipped around the mass of the shadow. Two arms rose from the depths, each sporting five gnarled and pointed fingers. The arms fidgeted and twisted like a stop-motion animation missing a few frames. Latte jumped off the bed and hid inside his litter box.

Megumi gripped her comforter as if it was a life preserver. Her nails bit her palms even through the blanket.

The woman-thing spoke, but Megumi couldn't understand what she was saying. It was Japanese. The dialect was what she had heard only in movies about samurai and geisha and castles and lords. This was not the tongue for discussing fashion and the new bakery down the street. She made out a few words such as "mine" and "taken." That was enough. That was all she ever wished to hear or know from that voice, sweet and calm though it was.

The woman began weeping. Her voice changed from gentle to rough. Her volume rose and Megumi could understand that she was asking a question. Something banged against the window. The sound jolted her to her senses. Megumi jumped out of the bed and turned around.

She expected nothing to be there, just like a scary movie. The fake out of a cat jumping out of the closet before the scares got too intense. She wished she was in a horror movie.

The woman was at the window. Megumi could see her haggard and hanging face with the loose tongue. The woman banged against the glass with her fist.

Again came the words "mine" and "taken" and a possible "give me."

Megumi stood still—mostly, if it weren't for her shaking and her whimpering.

The woman disappeared. There was no fading away, no slow receding like the mist at sunrise. She was just gone.

Then came the screaming. Wailing. Lamenting that tore through the walls of her apartment.

Megumi double checked that her door was locked. As fierce as it was, the crying didn't sound malevolent to her. It was filled with a pain that cut through her, both to marrow and to atom. Megumi cowered in a corner of the room. Latte wouldn't come near her. She sat in that corner, shivering and wide eyed, until the sun rose.

Only then did the screaming stop.

Two days passed by. Megumi fell asleep at work on that first afternoon. Caught a solid hour in the back before Reina noticed. She didn't sleep at all that night. The screaming continued from after sunset to sunrise. Her front door handle rattled, and something banged against it. The inside lock fluttered as if touched by an invisible hand.

The second day was even worse. She could see the woman out of the corner of her eye. At all times of day. No matter where she went. When

Megumi went to look at her, she was gone. The woman appeared in the bath next to her. She was standing behind a set of skirts at work. She lurked in the dark corners of every alleyway and every corner of every room. At times her image stayed as if burned on the inside of her eyelids.

The second night Megumi's mind almost snapped. Things escalated beyond the screaming and the rattling of the locks and the just out of sight stalking. The woman appeared at her window and actually opened it. Megumi rushed over and slammed it shut. Then the front door lock unlatched, and it opened. She saw a putrid leg clothed in a blood-stained robe step into her apartment. Megumi flew at the door and shut it on the woman.

It seemed that even though she could be in Megumi's line of sight at all times, the woman couldn't pass through solid objects. That's what Megumi silently prayed was true.

After shutting the door, it was no longer the woman that Megumi heard. The cries that rattled the walls were that of a baby. The hysterical screaming brought her mind back to the delivery table. Painted in her postpartum hemorrhage. The shrill monotone beep of the machine.

The thing that disturbed her the most though, was the progression. Night one was a banging at the window. Night two was the undoing of the locks. Night three was the woman opening entrance points and trying to come in. What would happen on night four?

Megumi's sleep deprived mind latched onto these thoughts as she got out of the bus in Miyama Village and walked toward her father's house. The tiny mountain hamlet was serene. No wind blowing. A clear and cloudless sky. Thatched roofed homes, rice paddies, and rolling hills surrounding it all. A single creek, overflowing due to the recent rains, raced through the center of the village.

She walked past her father's open gate and up to the front door. She
rang the bell and waited. Her eyes stung and her eyelids were weighing
down. She felt like vomiting and could hardly hold onto a clear concrete
thought. She had no one else to run to. No friends that would take her
seriously. And Dad was always a believer in the supernatural. Maybe he
would know something.

The door opened.

Dad was dressed in a green wool vest and dark brown slacks two sizes
too big for him. His bald head was edged with fluffy gray hair. His small
and powerful spectacles made his actual eyes seem even smaller than they
really were. Megumi took the moment in, stunned at how much smaller
her father seemed since, when was it, three years now?

"Hi Dad."

"Hi."

A moment of stilted silence.

"You want to come in?"

"Yes, thank you."

Dad led her inside and offered her a cup of tea. She waited in the living
room, sitting at a table. The light was dim inside. The windows were
small, and Dad didn't like to flip on the lights until it got dark. It was
musty and smelled of mildew. Dust specs floated around the cluttered
living room; piles of clothes, even a bicycle though it was missing one
tire. She laughed at how similar they were, neither of them could ever
clean up well.

Dad came in with a tea tray that shook in his hands.

"Thanks," she grabbed a cup and took a sip. "The place, it looks, nice."

He hummed a response in his throat that Megumi knew to be a "thank
you" or possibly an "I know."

Her father raised her by himself for most of her life. She had no memories of her mother since she died sometime when Megumi was a baby. Never got a straightforward explanation from Dad and she knew she may never get one.

He sat down. "So, uh," his eyes wandered around the room. "You said you wanted to talk?"

She gripped the table's edge tightly. It was smooth but felt like she might get a splinter if she held onto it harder. "I've been, this is difficult to say, I've been seeing something. A dead woman with a baby. She's been coming to me for three nights now. And I know you've always believed in this stuff, and I'm just scared, I don't know what to do."

Before speaking she felt like she was leaning off the side of a cliff. Now that the impossible was said, she waited for the impact.

Dad cleared his throat and put his cup down, looking down at his feet.

"By a river?' He asked.

"Y-yes, how did you know that?"

"You never got to know your mother. She used to pick these nice little Chrysanthemums and lay them by your crib. She used to think it would protect you from bad health."

"Dad, what does this—"

"Just listen. She died when you were still a baby. But you know what happened right after? I'd find those flowers in your room. Every single night for almost four years. I never doubted that it was her spirit looking after you. She was an Ubume. It's a, uh, ghost or spirit I think, of a woman who dies in or after childbirth. I thought it was fine at first. I mean, she was your mother. But as the years passed, she started getting violent. I would wake up in the middle of the night and see fresh cuts on your arms. Soon the flowers stopped coming but the cuts and bruises on you, and then on me, grew more frequent. You remember Saito-san, right? He told me this and took me to a temple to ask the monk more about it. We did a ritual, the poles and sheet down by the creek. We washed an incantation off the sheet and into the water and her spirit was saved from hell."

Megumi wanted to write this off as a fairy tale. As a warped mind clinging to a fiction. But her father wasn't a liar and wasn't losing his mind, as far as she could tell. After what she had seen by the river, she was open to believing.

"Dad, why didn't you ever tell me any of this about Mom? And Hell?"

"Why do you think I never told you? It wouldn't have done you any good to know, would it? And the monk, I forget his name, nice man. It was Tachibana or Takano or something." His eyes wandered off again. Scanning the walls of the home. Searching for something Megumi could never hope to relate to. "Sorry, what were we talking about?"

"Hell. Ubume."

"Yes, yes. The monk said that women who die without raising their children properly go to the Hell of Blood. Like a lake of blood, they get dipped into over and over again. You ...understand why it's blood?"

She nodded. Delivery table. Red and white. Monotone beep.

"That's horrible," she said. "Why punish them for something so stupid? It's not like they did anything wrong." She felt the fire rise up from her belly and into her throat.

Dad raised his hands up in defense. "I know, I know. This is what the monk said so who knows if it's true or not. But all I know is that the flowers stopped coming when we did the ritual. And I don't know why, but the people from Miyama see Ubume often."

She let out a sigh. A release valve to the hot pressure. "If that was Mom, she was being kind to me. The woman I've been seeing is..." Tears welled up in her eyes. "She's monstrous. And why me? Why is she coming after me!?"

"Some Ubume, the ones that lose their children, so not just the mother dying, they are searching for someone to take care of their baby. This drives them insane. They are very dangerous. Their anger is a poison that infects everything around them. Maybe you paid her attention and that's why? Or maybe it's because of the baby—" His face shriveled into itself. Megumi knew her father didn't bring up her stillbirth on purpose, but still, those words were a buzz saw to her heart.

Dad's face twitched. Almost like he was about to cry. Something she had never seen him do. She grabbed his hand and squeezed it. She smiled, as painful as it was to do so. His face relaxed and he nodded.

"You need to do the ritual. And whatever you do, do not pick up her baby. That's how she'll drag you down to hell with her. I'll call Saito-san and see what we can do."

"Dad, it has to be tonight. If we don't," she trailed off, thinking about that dead foot that breached her doorway the night before. One more night. One more step inside. In the corner of her vision just then, she noticed her. Sitting in a dark corner of the living room, behind the single tire bike. Holding the bundle to her exposed breast, her flesh sagging in decomposition. She was rocking back and forth and humming a lullaby Megumi didn't know. She did her best not to look at the woman but kept her eyes on her father.

"Okay, okay. He's retired and got nothing to do. We're old and rusty, but at least we have time." He chuckled, inviting her to do the same with his eyes.

Megumi didn't have the heart to try.

Night was almost here. Megumi, her father, Saito-san, and another elderly man—a Buddhist monk—stood on the banks of the river by her apartment. Dark clouds were gathering overhead, and the low rumbling of thunder spoke of horrors to come.

Megumi watched as her father and Saito-san hammered the four wooden poles into the ground. They wouldn't let her help.

The monk, she never caught his name, busied himself by writing characters onto a white sheet with his brush dipped in glistening ink. She could read some of the words. They were ethereal and muddled to her. Phrases like "form is emptiness, emptiness is form" and "release from attachment."

Dad and Saito-san finished setting up the poles, each one slightly shorter than they were, and helped the monk drape the sheet up and between them like a tent covering, fastening the sheet with rope to the poles. Her father slipped once while lifting up the sheet and Megumi feared he would fall and break his hip. She heard that Saito-san's wife died that way a year ago.

They finished erecting the structure beside the river and the monk began chanting his sutra as he gathered water from the river in a jug and then poured it over the sheet. The fresh ink ran down the white sheet and flowed into the river. She was told that this was symbolic of the Ubume's earthly attachments and desires being released and purified. No matter how much water was poured on that sheet, a faint ashy black stain remained. She couldn't help but think about the delivery table sheets and wonder if the nurses ever got her blood out of them.

Was that what happened to her? A purification of her desire to have a little girl to hold and love? Purification not in water and prayer but in blood and death.

Bitterness swallowed her mind. Would she, too, be tossed into the Hell of Blood? And for what? Not bringing a life into this world? If this was true of the spirit that stalked her, then she deserved pity, not fear. She deserved vengeance, not salvation.

The monk stopped chanting. "The ceremony is finished. The Ubume has been appeased."

Saito-san bowed his head in agreement. Her father smiled slightly.

"How can we know for sure?" She asked.

The monk smiled with no evidence that it touched his eyes, "Because the mantra never fails. Thank you for your time. Ah, Tanaka-san, about my payment?"

Dad took an envelope out of his jacket pocket and handed it to the monk.

The men packed up Saito-san's truck and, aside from her father, they drove off. Megumi agreed to let her Dad stay the night, his insistence, just to be sure.

As they both walked into the apartment, Megumi knew the ritual didn't work.

The woman was there. Across the river. Watching them.

Dad was asleep in Megumi's bed. She was sitting down on a futon she laid out for herself on the floor. Wide awake, petting Latte who had fallen asleep on her lap.

Rain had been falling for at least an hour. Megumi bit her lower lip as she searched the internet for more information about the Ubume. There were other rituals that could be performed. But if the sheet rite didn't work, she had no time or trust in the others to try them out.

She remembered her father saying, "Do not hold her baby". According to ChatGPT, the purveyor of all wisdom, if she did so, the baby would grow heavier and heavier until it dragged her down to hell. And if you refused to hold the baby? Depending on the Ubume in question, she might just murder you on the spot.

What was there to do?

The screaming began. There was no more time to think.

Her father did not wake up. It suddenly dawned on her tired brain that no one in her building was ever bothered by the screaming. Only she could hear it. But she heard it even before going to the woman and paying attention to her. Was Megumi marked from the beginning? And why did it all start now?

The shadow of the woman filled the window frame. Even behind the curtain Megumi could see her rotting flesh. Could smell the sour rancid meat. The woman's now red eyes stared deep into Megumi's. She held the bundle, the child, in front of the glass. And then smacked it against the window.

Still her father did not wake up. Megumi knew he would be of no help. He wouldn't even be able to see her. What would happen if she came inside?

The window flew open. Her front door slammed against the wall and Megumi saw that it too had been opened.

Looking from window to door, the woman was in both places at the same time. In both places offering the dead child up to Megumi. She took a step through the threshold of the door. Her rotten foot kicked the Crocs out of the way. At the window, she placed a rotting foot on the sill, the other came down next to her father's head on the pillow. Megumi saw the impression of her foot on the pillow. She wasn't just a spirit. She had weight. The next foot would come down on her father's head.

Megumi made a choice. She turned toward the door and walked forward to meet the woman who was now fully inside the apartment, hoping this would stop what was happening at the window.

The woman stopped crying. She jerked her head side to side as if her neck was broken. She stepped closer with the bundle raised.

Megumi was going to name her daughter Sora. She was going to teach her piano, take her to France, hold her hand on her wedding day. Now she was going to hold someone else's child.

Megumi reached out her hands.

The woman's face, up until now grotesque, seemed to soften. The red in her eyes gave way to white. The open sores closed up. The loose tongue was now held up by a lower jaw that appeared from nothing. With each step forward, the woman gained an ounce of life back. The smell of rot became thinner the closer she got. By the time she reached Megumi, so close that they could touch, the woman did not look dead, she looked alive. Cheeks red and skin smooth. She looked sad and desperate. But alive.

She placed the bloody bundle into Megumi's hands.

And vanished into nothingness.

The baby remained. Bloody and dead and rank. It started crying. Its stiff rigor mortis limbs thrashed about. It grew heavy in Megumi's hands. She tried to let go. To let the bundle roll off her hands. But it was glued to her. Megumi fell to her knees. Fire burned in her elbows and forearms. Her hands fell to the floor, still holding the child. She tried to lift them up but couldn't. She raised her hips in the air and pressed her feet into the ground and pulled with all her might.

Something in her elbow popped. A crack appeared on the floor. She noticed Latte nearby, watching her. Meowing gently, unsure of what was happening, only knowing Megumi was in distress.

Megumi yelled and screamed. Something she had never done in her life before. Years of pain unleashed in a moment of primal agony. All she could hear in her mind was that damn monotone beep. She pulled harder. And screamed louder.

To her left, a crack opened in the floor, red light shone forth. It split wider. What should have been room 204 below her was now a pool of blood. She saw writhing things in that thick red water. They were screaming. All of them women.

Then she felt rough hands grabbing her own. It was her father. He was down on his knees in front of her, trying to wedge his arthritic hands under hers, but he couldn't. They locked eyes and she could see the tears streaming down his face.

Her hands burned. Her heart ached. The pain of a thousand losses piled up in her. A voice came into her mind.

Let go. Be free of the pain. And fall into me.

The pool of blood growled. It was hungry. And it wanted her.

She knew in her gut then that if she let go, the thing in her hands would let her do so. But that would mean she'd join those down below.

Her father pressed his hands more firmly into hers and shouted. He yelled with what little voice he had. She had never heard him raise his voice. Like father, like daughter. They both held on. She could see that it was hurting him too. The bundle lit on fire. The "baby" wailed and kicked its flaming appendages. Megumi's hands were scorched. Pain like none she had experienced before. The fires burned her father's hands too.

Still, they held on. Still, they screamed together.

Megumi felt another pair of hands cover hers. Soft hands. Small hands. She heard a woman scream with them. Not the Ubume. A woman's voice she had heard once before on a VHS tape her Dad showed her of his wedding day.

And then it was gone. The bundle. The crack in the floor. The pool of blood. The woman's unseen hands.

Dad was on his ass, covered in sweat, his hands a bloody and burned mess. So were hers.

She embraced her father, and he embraced her. She clung to his neck and sobbed. He joined in.

Latte pushed his body between them and nuzzled their faces.

The rain stopped.

All was quiet.

AFTERWORD

T hank you for reading my first short story anthology. This project
was born out of my inability to relax. I had just finished writing
Under the Amber Wave in my Black Sun series and had to wait two
months for it to come out. During this time I was tempted to just not
write anything at all but decided, "Fuck it, let's try some short stories." All
of these stories were written in that two month time frame and I wanted
to experiment. Try out new points of view and even types of horror I
wasn't comfortable with writing.

For a first in my life I wrote in the first person. *Fried Rice* is a man's
written account about a strange woman he keeps on seeing at the local
store. *Longing* is from the point of view of the entity, the horror, that is
central to that story. Both of these were fun as I tried to get into these
"people's" heads. Both of these were created out of a spot of creative
bankruptcy. I had no ideas and zero drive to write. So I started looking
around, chose a random object (fried rice) and tried to make it scary.
Longing was a bit more personal since I wanted to try and tell a horror
story from the monster's eyes. For some reason I empathized with that
character for more than with the man in *Rice*.

Tornaq is based off a supposedly real story. A village near Anjikuni
Lake, in 1930 Nunavut, Canada, disappeared overnight. There's a lot

of evidence now that this never really happened but it was enough of a launchpad for my imagination. I love the arctic horror *The Terror* and found inspiration there.

The Face is intensely personal. My home has a glass door looking at the backyard, and beyond that, a dark Japanese forest. One of my most primal fears is that, when I pull back the curtains at night, a face is going to be there to greet me.

Foundations is a companion story to an upcoming novel of mine: *The Dead Roots of the Earth*. This will be the fourth book in the Black Sun series set to be released Fall 2025. You can probably tell from the short story that the overall narrative is an apocalyptic one. It shows what is happening in Tokyo during a cataclysmic event. The novel will flesh this out more.

The Man with the Glass Bones was my attempt at quiet horror. Of course, I can't be quiet for too long, hence the ending. I had just listened to the No Sleep story *Borrasca,* which involves kids in a small town and an urban legend. I took that basic premise and created my own take on small town American folk horror mixed with some Nordic myth.

The White Feather Club is based off of a Japanese legend about a nine-headed serpent deity that required the sacrifice of women to appease it. The main character works at a Japanese hostess club, which is a place men go to drink and flirt with pretty women. I thought the idea of offering women up to a demon fit that profession.

Fish Hooks is another one of my more apocalyptic stories. This idea has actually been in my head for the past year. I imagined my own version of a world ending invasion and, for some odd reason, the angler fish popped up in my head. Of course a more eldritch version of them.

Smile Wide for Me started as a simple stalker story when I first wrote it. No ghosts or monsters, just human evil. But as I wrote it, the woman in that story became a serial killer in my mind. Don't ask me, I just obey the voices in my head in the moment. I thought it would be fun to for the "scary paranormal" aspect to not be the monster here.

Daughter of Spring was an experiment with grief and healing. I don't know if you liked it, but this one is my favorite. The idea that the ghost in the tale is here to help, that loved ones don't leave us, and that there are truly evil things out in the woods, is just perfect to me. It's also loosely based off of a Greek myth. For all you nerds out there, Google the name "Cora" and find out what that is in Greek.

The Thing in the Closet is weird. You may have noticed. I wanted to focus on disgust as the source of fear. And this story is just where my mind went. The idea that there is this entity that can reduce you to your absolute lowest state, both physically and mentally, is scarier than death.

Pitter-Patter Go the Feet was born out of my childhood fear of the *Cat's Eye* movie. Remember that little demon gnome that comes out of the little girl's wall? Yeah. Pure nightmare fuel. Fun fact: the man who played the demon went to my church back in California. Met him once and didn't even cry.

Lastly, *Ubume.* To date, this is the only time I have cried while writing a story. I didn't expect the ending (for short stories I never plot that far). The folklore is real as well. The Ubume is a Japanese spirit and most of what I wrote about is part and parcel of its legend. I embellished some aspects: the dragging people to hell mainly. But not the Pool of Blood unfortunately.

I sincerely hoped you found some stories to love here. My plan is to write two anthologies like this every year. For how many years? Well, as long as I still enjoy writing.

Please consider leaving a review on Amazon or Goodreads since that helps to support my writing. It lets me know that I should keep on going!

You can also sign up for my newsletter at my website: shawnbrookswri
tes.com

Memento Mori,

Shawn

A REQUEST

I f you found this set of horrors entertaining, please consider leaving me a review! Reviews are what makes or breaks an indie author's career. By reviewing, you help support me to keep on doing this. The QR codes below are for my Goodreads page and for the US Amazon store to leave a review. If you would like to review on other country's Amazon stores this code will not take you there.

Thank you again!

US Amazon Store

Goodreads

SHAWN BROOKS

Printed in Great Britain
by Amazon

56916602R00117